# BEE FRIEND

Written by A.R. Johnson

Illustrated by Marian Gorin

Published in 2021



Printed in the United States of America

Editing by Melanie Lopata ~ Get It Write (www.getitwriteeditingco.com)

# ACKNOWLEDGEMENTS

My aunt, Augusteen, told me as a kid that I could someday become an author after reading one of my short stories. Although it was a great compliment, I didn't really believe it, but I never forgot it. Thank you for planting the seed, Auntie!

The journey to get to this point has had its challenges, but it was well worth it. None of this would be possible without the support of my wife, Zaranda. You have been with me every step of the way. I'm so blessed to call you my wife. Thank you for your encouragement.

Nathan Wahl and Kevin Kringle—you two were the first to encourage me to pursue my dream. I don't think you two realized how much I needed it. Thank you; I really appreciate the both of you.

I would like to extend my best regards to Andy Kooyenga. You read the first three chapters of my manuscript to your daughter, and she loved it. Thank you for taking time out of your busy schedule to read it.

Roxy Carrington, you read the entire manuscript. Your honest assessment meant a lot to me. You were one of the first who made me believe that I could really accomplish my dream of becoming an author. From the bottom of my heart, thank you.

Momma Jan and Sharon Goldsmith—I appreciate you both for believing in me and encouraging me to write. Your support is one of the main reasons I'm an author today.

Rachel Freeman and Isaiah Pickens—I'm so grateful that you let me use Isaiah to be Max. It really motivated me to finish the book. I appreciate the support from the both of you. Isaiah, you helped bring one of my main characters to life.

Marian Gorin, you are truly a very talented Illustrator! Your wonderful illustrations brought this story to life! To think I was almost convinced to publish this book without illustrations! I'm so glad I found you!

# DEDICATION

I loved you from the second I witnessed you opening your eyes. The moment I held you in my arms for the first time was the moment I knew I wanted to do something for you that would last beyond the both of us. Neriah Joanna Johnson, you had every part in the making of this book—more than anyone who gave input. You gave me ideas that I hadn't even thought of. You begged me every night to read my manuscript to you. I read you this story so much that even I was getting tired of it. Yet to you, every time I read it was like the first time. Your natural enthusiasm is the reason I believe this story will touch every child or adult that reads it. I envision you reading this to your children someday. You are my "why," Neriah. I had you on my mind as I wrote this book. I loved seeing your precious face light up when it was story time. It absolutely warmed my heart just to see you rush to bed and wait for me to read you a chapter before you went to sleep. You are the best daughter a father could ever ask for. I dedicate this book to you, Neriah. You are my heart, and I love you more than you could ever imagine!

# TABLE OF CONTENTS

# CHAPTER ONE

## A BEE'S LIFE

"Come on, Tank! Let's hurry up and finish so I can have some time to get my dandelion nectar," Dex called.

"Don't worry, Dex. You'll have plenty of time to gather some of your precious dandelion nectar," Tank replied. "Let's just make it back to the hive on time for a change. It's a new foraging year, and we are not coming back late like we did last year."

Dex and Tank were forager bees. The bees spent the entire fall and winter months living in their hive to avoid the cold. Now it was the forager bees' first few days out since last fall. Over the winter months, the bees' honey supply had been nearly depleted. The hive needed to make more honey. Dex and Tank's job was to gather nectar and pollen from flowers and bring it back to the hive to make more honey.

Dex loved to gather nectar from dandelions specifically. He thought it added a signature flavor to the hive's honey. Dex would usually go out of his way just to get dandelion nectar. He would go too far from their normal routes. He would even risk certain dangers at times just to make sure the hive's honey was made just right.

"Dex, we have two more houses left before we are done, and then we can get the dandelion you so desperately need to get," Tank said sarcastically.

"Let's pick up the pace, then," replied Dex.

Dex and Tank had been foraging together for as long as they could remember. They occasionally liked to call themselves "The Zoom and Boom Connection." Tank was the Boom because he was the bigger and stronger of the two. Tank also could carry more nectar and pollen because of his size. Dex was the Zoom because he was faster and could maneuver around better, which was why Dex tended to go out farther than he was supposed to, which caused him to get into trouble with the queen sometimes.

"Okay, Dex, we're done now. Let's head to the playground," Tank ordered.

"I'll race you there, slow poke!" shouted Dex, and he quickly flew off.

Dex buzzed loudly as he flew! He zigzagged past light poles and through parked bikes spokes; he breezed past fences and bushes, picket gate doors, and trees! Dex loved to fly fast; he knew he was good at it. In fact, Dex was the fastest bee in the entire hive. Dex flew upward and closed his compound eyes as the wind rushed across his face.

*This is the life,* Dex thought.

***

Tank was about a block behind, but he didn't care. He liked to take his time anyway. It was his time to take it all in. Sometimes, Tank would rest on top of a light pole in the neighborhood and watch the squirrels run up and down the trees. He would watch the bees from other hives go about their foraging duties. He would also watch the humans go in and out of their houses. The bees kept their distance from humans because humans were unpredictable. They would run from the bees, screaming; they would try to capture them to put them in jars; they would swat at them—or even worse, they would try to kill them. The bottom line for Tank was simple: Humans were NEVER to be trusted.

Tank caught up to Dex, who was waiting impatiently on the top of a picket fence.

"'Bout time you showed up," grumbled Dex.

"Whatever. You know the drill. You've got ten minutes. *GO!*" snapped Tank.

***

Dex had ten minutes to collect as much dandelion nectar as he possibly could. All the yards in the neighborhood were maintained consistently, so rarely did dandelions grow in the lawns. The only place Dex could collect a good amount of dandelion nectar was from an old playground nearby. This place was teeming with dandelions and was Heaven to Dex.

The playground was a virtual ghost town. Rarely did the children play there because of the indoor entertainment that arrived over the years, so the playground had become neglected. The slide had a thin brown layer of dirt on it. The chains on the swings were rusted. However, there was a lot of tall, neglected grass that was home to dozens of dandelions. More dandelions meant great tasting honey for the hive.

Dex had to hurry and collect as much dandelion nectar as he could. After ten minutes, Tank would leave, assuming that Dex perished. It was too dangerous at the playground for forager bees; too many predators roamed unbothered at the playground.

Spiders, birds, and wasps were natural enemies to them. Dex knew this and understood it. There was no need to risk both bees' lives for dandelion nectar. Tank would sit on the top step of the slide and wait while Dex foraged. Dex also understood why Tank could be on edge sometimes when they came to the playground. Tank didn't like the risks that Dex would take for the dandelion nectar. Tank was afraid he would lose his best friend.

"Four minutes, Dex!" shouted Tank. There was no answer and Tank grew anxious. Dex would normally take about five minutes. More time went by and still no sign of Dex. "Deeeeeeexxx!!!" Tank cried. "Two minutes!" Still, there was no answer.

Tank was starting to get worried. "Thirty seconds!" he yelled. By this time, Tank was spreading his wings for flight. In his mind, he was already back at the hive explaining to the queen that Dex was PWF - Perished While Foraging.

Tank was about to say "fifteen seconds" when he saw Dex zip out from the bushes. "Dex, I thought you were a goner!" cried Tank.

"I'm sorry," said Dex, panting loudly. "I went too far into the bushes and it was getting hard to hear you."

"I'm just glad that you're alright," said Tank. "Now that you are okay, I'm upset with you! This has gone far enough! You take too many risks just for stupid dandelion nectar! I thought you'd been eaten or something!"

"I'm sorry Tank," said Dex. "I thought I heard another bee's distress buzz further in the bushes, so I went to go check. But before I could get there, my time was almost up."

"Well, did you find the other bee?" asked Tank.

"No," said Dex. "I couldn't find him."

"Well, I'm sure he'll find his way out of there," said Tank. "And now we are going back to the hive late again. Let's go home. I'm sure the queen will be waiting for us now."

***

As Dex and Tank emptied their nectar and pollen back at the hive, one of the guard bees from the queen's throne approached them. "Your presence is required by the queen," he announced. "Come with me now."

At the queen's throne, Dex and Tank nervously stood. They didn't know what kind of mood she would be in. She could be "friendly upset" or she could be "angry upset."

All she did was look at them with concern on her face. Finally she spoke. "You two are starting this year off on the wrong foot by coming back late from your foraging assignments! Tank, explain yourselves!"

Just before Tank could speak, Dex jumped in and cut him off. "This was my fault, Your Majesty," said Dex. "I wanted to collect some dandelion nectar for our honey and I took too long and I—"

"Silence, Dex!" snapped the queen. "I asked *Tank* to speak, not you!" She looked at Tank and gestured for him to speak. All six of Tank's legs were shaking now. The queen was indeed "angry upset."

Safety was a major concern of the queen. She cared deeply for all the bees in her hive. It was her job as the queen to provide leadership, structure, safety, and a host of other things to the hive. She provided those things for the bees in every part of the hive: the foragers, the soldiers, the nursery, etc. Every bee in the hive respected the queen because the queen respected every bee in the hive.

Tank could understand why the queen would be very upset at them for constantly breaking the simple rule to come back on time. They were forager bees. Other than the scouts, they were the only bees that ventured off far away from the hive to collect nectar for honey every day. Because of the outside dangers, they didn't always come back.

"Your Majesty, our sincere apologies." Tank's voice trembled as he spoke. "We foraged, just as you asked. We had extra time so we went past our route to collect some dandelion nectar. It was at this time that Dex heard another bee's distress buzz in the bushes at the park."

"Is this true, Dex?" asked the queen.

"Yes, Your Majesty," replied Dex.

"This other bee," continued the queen. "Did you see him?"

"No," said Dex.

"Something about that doesn't seem right," the queen mused. "I would advise that you no longer visit that playground, Dex."

"But Your Majesty," Dex argued. "Dandelion nectar has improved the quality of our honey."

"It doesn't matter, Dex," the queen retorted. "Although dandelion nectar has improved the quality of our honey—and I do appreciate what you have done—it's just not worth your life."

"What about the distress buzz, Your Majesty?" asked Dex. "That bee needs our help."

"I don't like it one bit," said the queen, shaking her

head. “That playground is swarming with enemies that will do harm to our bees. The playground is now forbidden.”

“But—”

The queen interrupted. “I have spoken, and you both are dismissed.”

Tank turned and gave a scolding look at his best friend. Dex whispered, “I’m sorry, Tank.” The two friends left the queen’s throne and went to their quarters.

As Dex and Tank left, the queen was in deep thought about the distress buzzing in the bushes. She wondered what it could possibly be. After a few moments of thought, an alarmed look came across her face and she hopped up and hastily flew to her quarters.

***

Dex could not sleep that night. He kept thinking about that distress buzz in the bushes. He was over the dandelion nectar; a fellow bee needed his help. Besides, he had enough dandelion nectar stored away for at least a week.

Finally, Dex made up his mind. He was going to rescue that bee. He was going to go back to the playground one more time, but not for dandelion nectar. He was going on a search and rescue mission. Even if it went against the queen’s command, he was going to do it. Now he only had to convince his best friend, Tank, to go with him. He would worry about that part tomorrow. Finally, Dex went to sleep.

# CHAPTER TWO

## A STICKY SITUATION

NATURE'S SPRING SONG: The sun peeked over the horizon, being careful not to abruptly wake up the world. The spring air was very still and quiet. Too early for the gentle gust, it thought. The nighttime insects and animals, sensing their shift was ending, started their retreat to their burrows, trees, and underground homes for rest. The morning dew was sitting on the low-cut lawns in the neighborhood. On a nearby spider's web, some of the beads of moisture sparkled like clear, glossy pearls. The neighborhood was still and quiet, not ready to be awakened just yet. It was nature's time right then.

***

The spring air finally decided to contribute to nature's song and sent its gentle gusts through the trees. The leaves, longing for the morning breeze, swayed happily back and forth. The sun peaked higher over the horizon, as if to get a better feel for nature's song. For nature's song was not only heard; it was felt and it was experienced by those who truly appreciated it.

By now, the sun was over the horizon and the morning dew had almost evaporated. The gentle warmth of the sun was welcomed by the flowers, and they showed their appreciation by opening their petals wide to soak up what the sun had to offer.

That was the very moment when Dex and Tank would start their daily routine to forage for nectar in the neighborhood. Dex and Tank loved mornings; the nectar in the flowers was particularly sweet at that time. As they landed on each flower to collect the nectar and pollen, they would take a sip of the nectar. Each flower never disappointed. The taste was always perfect. That was the best job ever.

Being a forager had its advantages. All the bees in the hive had tasted nectar. However, to drink nectar out of a freshly opened flower was truly an experience that only a forager could appreciate. There were many dangers a forager bee could face—far more than any other bee at the hive - but sipping sweet, fresh nectar out of an open flower could sometimes make it all worthwhile.

Dex was nervous. All night he had been thinking about the other bee at the playground. He wondered if the bee had a broken wing, or maybe he was trapped somewhere, or perhaps he was sick. Either way, Dex had to find him. Dex was also nervous about breaking the news to Tank that he was going back to the playground - with or without him.

Finally, Dex could not contain his concern about the situation and he decided to let Tank know. They were both resting on a nearby branch in a tree when Dex gave out a long, slow sigh and spoke. "Tank, I'm going back to the playground," he said.

Tank, who was sipping on his nectar, coughed and nearly spit it out of his mouth. He turned and looked at Dex. "Are you kidding me?" he shouted. "Did you get your antennae crossed? The queen said the playground was off limits!"

"I know she said it's off limits," said Dex. "But that bee needs our help."

"Do you remember Tazz, Mace, and Dez?" asked Tank.

"Sure, I remember them," replied Dex.

"What do those bees have in common?" asked Tank. Dex sighed deeply with sorrow and answered, "They're all dead."

"All because they disobeyed the queen's safety regulations," added Tank. "Now, let's forget about that suspicious distress buzz and finish up. We're ahead of schedule for once."

Dex looked at Tank. He had expected Tank to disagree with him, but Dex was going to go to the playground with or without Tank. "I'm still going to the playground," he said.

Tank sighed. He knew Dex was going with or without him, and yet Tank saw something different in Dex. Helping this other bee really meant a lot to him. This was a selfless act that Dex really felt strongly about, even if it would possibly cost him his life. Tank did not want Dex to go back to the playground, but if he did go, Tank would be there to have his back.

Tank smiled at his friend. "You have ten minutes," he said.

After they were finished with their foraging duties, Dex and Tank made it to the playground.

"Well, here we are," said Tank.

"Yeah," sighed Dex.

Both were nervous. There was always tension when Dex foraged for dandelion nectar at the playground, but this was obviously different. Dex and Tank stood on the top step of the dirty slide. The bushes were behind the slide where Dex would enter.

They sat silently for a few seconds before Tank finally spoke. "Okay, Dex, you have ten minutes. Let's get this over with quickly. Find the other bee, if he's still alive, and bring him out."

"When I find him, I will let out a loud buzz," said Dex. Tank nodded.

Dex gathered his courage, opened his wings, took a deep breath, and flew into the thick bushes.

***

"This is it," Dex bravely declared.

The bushes were bunched together very tightly. It was dark, but still some daylight shone through. It was a sunny day, so Dex could see some beams of sunlight bouncing off the leaves. He ventured further in. He heard Tank yell out in the distance, "Eight minutes!" Tank couldn't see Dex. Dex was on his own now.

Finally, Dex made it to the spot where he first heard the distress buzz. He wondered if the bee was even alive at this point.

"Helloooo!" Dex cried. "Are there any bees in here? I heard your distress buzz. I'm here to rescue you!"

"Six minutes!" yelled Tank in the distance.

Dex barely heard him. Dex had never gone this far into the bushes before. He could see the other neighborhood from this side. He looked upward. The sun was shining brightly through a big hole at the top of the bushes. From Dex's view, it looked like a tunnel exit at the top of the bushes.

Then, suddenly, Dex heard the distress buzzing again! It was very loud this time!

**Buzzzz . . . buzzzz . . . . . . . . . Buzzzz . . . buzzzz.**

***

"Five minutes, Dex!" shouted Tank. Tank grew anxious. He couldn't see or hear Dex. Tank wanted to go in after him, but he knew if they were both to get in trouble, no other bees would be able to locate them. The best thing for Tank to do was to sit and wait.

***

Dex looked around but couldn't determine where the distress buzz was coming from. "Where are you?" he shouted. "Say something!" He heard the buzzing again. This time, Dex closed his eyes and focused with his hearing. "Ah! I have to go up!" he said. "He's at the top. I'll fly up to get a better look."

The opening was too bright for Dex to see. The sun beamed straight down into the opening; Dex had to squint his eyes really tight just to see well enough so he wouldn't hit any branches on the way up. The closer Dex got to the top, the brighter the opening got. Dex was practically flying blind.

***

"Two minutes, Dex!" shouted Tank. "Where are you, Dex?" he asked himself. Now Tank was regretting the decision to come back to the playground with Dex. He hovered back and forth, as if he was pacing. He was feeling worry, fear, and anger all at the same time.

***

Dex was near the opening, so he decided to slow down. He still couldn't see well because of the sunbeam. He was just at the top of the bushes when he suddenly felt something sticky strike his face. He then realized that he had the sticky stuff on his wings. He opened his eyes and noticed that he was suspended in mid-air on top of the bush. Dex looked left and right and gasped—

To his horror, Dex had flown headfirst into a spider's web!

Dex and Tank had only been informed and read about spiders in their foraging training. They knew how crafty and dangerous spiders could be, but they had never really encountered one up close. The only bees they had heard of that were caught in webs were spoken of in past tense, because none of them had survived. They only knew of one bee that was caught in a web before. That bee was lucky because the spider had abandoned the web. He had used his distress buzz and had later been rescued.

Now the only thing Dex had hoped for was that this web was also abandoned and that he could send out his distress buzz. As soon as this thought had crossed his mind, Dex felt a pluck at the web.

**Pluck . . . pluck . . . . . . . . . Pluck . . . pluck.**

Dex looked over, and there in the corner of the web stood a large black-and-yellow garden spider! He had black and yellow stripes on his eight long, slender legs and had black and yellow spots across his body. He had two large eyes that were surrounded by six little eyes, totaling eight overall. In addition, he was wearing a sly grin on his face that was spread from fang to fang.

As Dex gained his focus from the sunbeam, he could see the remains of other unfortunate insects that was scattered about.

*I should've listened to the queen,* thought Dex. He was now thinking about the other bees that had disobeyed the queen's orders in the past. It appeared that he was about to join them in death.

The spider moved in closer to get a better look at his prize. "One minute left," whispered the garden spider.

A surprised look came across Dex's face. The garden spider had heard Tank the past few days, yelling out how much time Dex had before he would leave. Dex started moving to free himself from the sticky web but he only became tangled more.

"That's right, bee," laughed the spider. "Keep struggling." The spider leaned in closer and counted down some more. "Five . . . four . . . three . . . two . . . one . . . zero," he taunted. "Your buddy should be leaving about now."

The spider was right. Tank, now in tears, had actually waited two extra minutes in hope that he would see Dex zooming out from the bushes.

"Dex!" he cried. "If you're in trouble, send out a buzz!" Nothing from Dex came from the bushes. "I have to go, Dex," sobbed Tank. He geared up his wings for flight, turned, and regretfully flew away.

***

The spider, who had scurried up on a higher branch in time to see Tank fly away, returned his attention to his newfound prize catch.

"Where's the other bee?" Dex interrogated. "Did you eat him?"

"Eat?" replied the spider, shaking his head. "I don't eat; I drink. To answer your question: there are no other bees here. You just fell for my distress buzz call from my web. I've studied the bees I've caught in the past."

The spider grabbed a few strands of his web and plucked at them. The strands vibrated back and forth. The spider tightened the strands while they vibrated which gave off a perfect replication of a distress buzz.

Dex grew sick when he heard it. He knew he had fallen victim to a crafty scheme devised by the spider.

"You guys are so hard to catch," said the garden spider. "You are the first bee I have caught using this method! Bees are my favorite." The spider was now rubbing his front two legs together slowly. "You guys have a unique flavor that's different from other insects I have caught."

The spider, hovering just above Dex, looked with a "far away" gaze in his eight eyes. He tasted the air, as if he was savoring a lost flavor. Then he looked back at Dex. "Bees have a sweet flavor about them," he said. "Perhaps it's because of that honey you all make. I guess it is . . . in your blood. It has been so-o-o-o-o long since I've had a sweet bee visit my web. Flies, cockroaches, and beetles are too salty . . . YUCK! Grasshoppers, crickets, and earwigs . . . too gritty."

The spider continued, "Ants? Ants are good, but do you know how many of those little suckers I have to catch just to get a satisfying meal?" The spider inched closer to Dex. "Your large friend would've lasted me at least a week if I had caught him," he said. "But you will suffice."

Although Dex remained trapped in the web, he could still move a bit. The garden spider, still gloating about his catch, had forgotten about Dex's stinger. The garden spider was close, but Dex needed the right angle to strike. When Dex saw his chance, he quickly swung his stinger in the direction of the garden spider.

He missed.

The garden spider, realizing a close call, breathed a sigh of relief. "You feisty little bee!" he screamed. Then, he quickly composed himself. "Ah, ah, aaaahhh," he said calmly, while waving one of his front legs from side to side.

"I see I haven't been a good host with my excessive talking. Well, I guess I'll just 'wrap' this conversation up." The garden spider began to wrap Dex with more of his sticky webbing. Dex knew a bite from the spider would spell imminent doom for him.

The garden spider was singing and spinning web, wrapping Dex ever so tightly. He was about to bite Dex, when a butterfly slammed into his web.

"Oh my, this is my lucky day!" exclaimed the garden spider. "I love butterflies! They are so-o-o buttery," he joked. "Now, you stay put right there. Don't go anywhere," said the garden spider sarcastically. "I have to go wrap up my dinner. You will be dessert later." The garden spider scurried off to wrap up the butterfly and left Dex trapped in a spool of sticky webbing.

Dex began to sob. He knew he was about to be PWF. In addition, he was completely helpless, and he knew that no other bees were coming to his rescue. A feeling of despair came over Dex, and he continued to sob bitterly.

# CHAPTER THREE

## A HUMAN'S POINT OF VIEW

"Hurry up and come downstairs, Max," Mrs. Thomas called. "It's Monday. Time for school!"

Max, still in bed, pulled the covers over his head. "Ugh, I don't wanna get up, Mom," he moaned and quickly went back to sleep. However, within a few moments, the smell of smoked bacon filled his room. Although Max tried to sleep through the smell, he just couldn't resist, so finally he got out of bed, washed up, and went downstairs to eat.

"Good morning, Mom," greeted Max as he kissed his mom on the cheek.

"Good morning, Max."

Max joined the table where his dad and sister were already sitting. "Good morning, family!" Max exclaimed with enthusiasm.

"Wow, you sure are excited this morning," Mr. Thomas mused as he sipped on his coffee.

"Too excited on a Monday," Joanna, his younger sister, grumbled. "He's going to ask for something. Just watch."

"Can I not be excited on a Monday without asking for something in particular?" asked Max.

"No," replied Mr. Thomas.

"Well, I feel like it's going to be a great day for me," said Max.

Soon the table went quiet. The only sounds made now were the utensils clanging on their plates as the family ate breakfast: scrambled cheese eggs with sautéed mushrooms, oven-baked hickory-smoked bacon that was crisped to perfection, steel cut oats with maple syrup and brown sugar, English muffins with butter and strawberry preserves, and fresh squeezed orange juice.

"Cora, you did it again," said Mr. Thomas. "Breakfast was delicious."

"Thank you, Hon," Mrs. Thomas smiled.

Max got up from the table and put his dish in the sink. As he passed Joanna, he gave a slight tug on her ponytail.

"Stop pulling my hair, you clown!" she yelled.

"Make me," Max sneered jokingly. He turned to walk away but Joanna quickly turned around and kicked his leg causing him to stumble, and he fell with a thud.

"Nice trip! See ya next fall," Joanna laughed.

"That's enough!" snapped their father.

"But Daddy, Max started it!" Joanna cried.

"I said that's enough," Mr. Thomas repeated.

Both kids quickly calmed down, and Joanna grabbed her things and headed to her dad's car in the garage. "Later, Mom," she said as she kissed her mother on the cheek.

Mr. Thomas followed Joanna out to the car. "See you tonight, Hon," he said, kissing his wife.

Max's school was only a few blocks away, so there was no rush, but he decided to get to school early that morning. "Leaving for school, Mom," he said. "Love you." Max kissed his mother and he was off to school.

Mrs. Thomas had the entire house to herself now. "Ahhhh, the quiet," she sighed. She went to the living room, sat on the couch, stretched her feet on the ottoman, and took a quick nap.

***

Max was still on his way to school when his day began to sour. First, he realized he had left his homework at home and he was too far away to go back without being late. Later, at school, he was caught talking during study time, so he had to serve a detention after school (followed by a call home). By the time Max was sitting in detention, his enthusiasm for a great day had vanquished. To top off his now bad day, that call home about his detention meant he would not be allowed to go outside to play after school. He would have to stay inside the rest of the day.

Max was so bummed out about his day that he decided to take a different route home. He thought a change in scenery would lift his spirits and help him forget the bad day.

On the way home on his new route, Max picked up a stick and took occasional swipes at the bushes as he passed them. On the last block, Max was on his normal path home. He was walking by a familiar path of bushes when he heard a dull, muffled buzz. He stopped, looked in, and saw a bee trapped in a spider's web.

He ignored the trapped insect and proceeded to walk away. Max was only a few steps away when he stopped, sighed, and glanced slightly back in the direction of the trapped bee. "I'm having a bad day," he told himself. "But that bee is having a far worse day than I am."

Max turned completely around and ran back to the spider's web. By now, the bee was completely wrapped in a cocoon of web. Max also noticed that a butterfly was now in the web.

***

The spider was just about to start wrapping up the butterfly when he noticed a huge brown stick coming at his web. The spider appeared to have an incredulous look on his face, as if to say, "You've got to be kidding me."

With a quick flick of Max's stick, the butterfly was now free. She landed a few inches away from the web, cleaned off the remaining web on her wings, and flew away.

The spider, knowing this was not going to end well for him, still had one last shot at salvaging his stashed bee. He quickly scurried across his failing web to collect his wrapped bee. Suddenly, his path was blocked by Max's stick. With another quick flick, the spider was sent flying into the air. He landed on the ground on the other side of the bushes and retreated beneath the bushes.

***

Max carefully used his stick to pick up the wrapped bee and placed him on the ground. He wondered if he was too late with his rescue because the bee lay motionless. Max slowly undressed the bee's cocoon of webbing to give him room to move. Max was cautious because he didn't want to get stung by the bee. He stood back a few feet to give the bee some room and waited for some sign of life from him.

Suddenly, the bee started to buzz! He was alive!

"There you go, lil' buddy," Max said. "You're free now."

The bee walked around for a few seconds as if to gather his thoughts. Then he spread his wings and quickly flew away.

# CHAPTER FOUR

## HOME AGAIN

Tank hurried back to the hive. He didn't empty his pollen and nectar; he flew directly to the queen's throne room.

"Your Majesty," he said, panting. "Dex is PWF!"

"What happened?" the queen asked calmly.

"We were foraging, and Dex wanted to rescue the other bee!" said Tank.

The queen quickly stood up from her throne and gave Tank an angry glare. *"YOU WHAT??!!"* she bellowed.

"It was his idea, Your Majesty," explained Tank. "I only went with him to back him up."

"You two blatantly disobeyed a direct order that I just declared yesterday!" shouted the queen. "We've just lost Dex because you two decided not to listen to me!" She turned to her guards. "Seize him!" she ordered.

Two guard bees came over and escorted Tank away to the detention cell.

***

Meanwhile, Dex was on his way back to the hive. He was still processing all the events that had happened to him. He landed in a flower garden on a windowsill to drink some nectar.

*That boy saved my life,* thought Dex. *Why did he do it? Humans are normally mean to us insects.*

Dex was grateful for his second chance at life, but he knew he had to go back to the hive to face the queen's potential punishment. He figured that, by now, Tank would have given his report about him being PWF. He also knew that the queen would be very upset with Tank. It was important that he get back to the hive as soon as possible.

He also couldn't wait to tell the hive what had just happened to him. He had been trapped in a spider's web that had a real spider in it, and he had lived to tell about it. He sipped a little more nectar from the flower and flew away to the hive.

***

Back at the hive, the queen was still upset about what had happened to Dex. She was also thinking about Tank; she was worried about him. She thought that she had been too harsh on him because he had disobeyed her orders. After all, he had just lost his best friend and then she'd had him detained. The queen's heart softened and she went to talk to Tank in his detention cell.

"Hello, Tank," the queen said softly. Tank stood up and greeted the queen. "I can't imagine how difficult this day has been for you. Please accept my sincere apologies for disregarding your feelings. I am sorry about the loss of your friend. How are you holding up?"

"I'm not doing too well right now," Tank replied. "Your Majesty, what are you doing down here?"

"Tank, I'm afraid I have some bad news about what happened to Dex," the queen said. "I believe Dex was tricked by a spider."

"A spider?" asked Tank.

"Yes," replied the queen. "After I dismissed you two yesterday, I was pondering over the distress buzz Dex had told me about coming from the bushes. I went to my library and followed up on my studies of spiders, and, to my surprise, I found that spiders can also mimic our distress buzz."

Tank's heart dropped and he grew weak when he heard this. He then became very angry. "So, you're telling me that my best friend was tricked and later devoured by a low-life spider?" he asked.

"I'm afraid so, Tank," replied the queen. "I wanted to tell you both, but I had already commanded you not to go back to the playground. I was going to tell you both today about the spider mimics then you showed up and told me you both had gone back there, and now Dex is PWF. I got upset and I had you detained."

"My apologies for disobeying your command, Your Majesty," said Tank.

"In my opinion, Tank, you did the right thing by going with Dex," said the queen. "Dex was brave to go rescue a fellow bee, and you were brave to go with him because you cared for him. However, there is a reason why I am the queen. In the future, I expect you to obey my orders."

"Will do," replied Tank.

The queen motioned to the guard bee to release Tank. As they were walking back to her throne room, another guard bee flew up to the queen. He had a surprised look on his face, and he was out of breath.

"Speak," the queen ordered.

"Your Majesty, you are not going to believe this," he said, still panting. "But one of our foragers just came back to the hive. It's Dex, and he's waiting in your throne room!"

The queen and Tank looked at each other, and they both flew quickly to her throne room.

Dex sat looking worn out and tired, and he still had a few traces of webbing on his furry body. He was exhausted mentally, but he appeared to be in good spirits.

Tank flew over as fast as he could to meet his best friend and they shared a long embrace.

"Dex . . . I thought you were . . . How did you . . . ?" Tank was so excited; he couldn't get a straight sentence out.

The queen stayed behind and smiled. She loved to witness moments like this with her bees. It showed a sense of togetherness and solidarity that she wanted her hive to have with one another. There was no need for her to punish Dex now. She was just glad to see him back home alive. Besides, experience was the best teacher on this day.

"Your Majesty," Dex said. "I am so sorry I disobeyed you."

"You are forgiven," replied the queen. "I'm just glad you are back in one piece."

"I have so much to tell you, My Queen," said Dex. "I was tricked by a spider and was trapped in his web!"

Tank looked at the queen with amazement. She had just told him that earlier.

"How did you escape?" asked the queen.

"The spider was about to bite me, but a butterfly landed in the web too!" Dex replied. "Then I was rescued . . . BY A HUMAN!"

Every bee in the queen's throne room let out a collective gasp.

"A *human*?" asked the queen.

"Yes, a human," said Dex excitedly. "He used a stick to rescue me and the butterfly!"

One of the queen's servants brought over some fresh nectar for Dex and he drank all of it. He continued, "The human spoke to me after he freed me."

"What did he say?" asked Tank.

"He told me I was free, and he called me buddy!" Dex replied. "Then I flew away as fast as I could."

"Sounds like you had a very close call with two of our well-known enemies," said Tank. "I'm glad you're alive to tell your story."

"Well, I think that is enough excitement for the day everyone," said the queen. "Let's regroup and prepare for tomorrow."

The queen gave Dex and Tank the next day off, as she figured they needed it after their trying ordeal.

Both bees went to their quarters for some well-deserved rest.

# CHAPTER FIVE

## THE ENCOUNTER

Dex was restless later that night. He kept thinking about lying trapped in the spider's web. He thought about the smell of it as he had lain wrapped up. He thought about that bragging spider. *He was so arrogant,* Dex thought.

He thought about the boy who had rescued him and how friendly he had been to him when he had freed him.

All these thoughts were racing through Dex's mind, and it caused him to become very restless. Dex really wanted to find the boy and thank him, but he knew that bees do not speak to humans. In fact, animals and insects only communicated to humans through their natural language: barking, meowing, chirping, etc. Dex wanted to speak actual words to the boy. He didn't want to tell Tank of his intentions because he knew Tank would be strongly against it.

Early morning before sunrise, Dex was walking about through the hive when he came across a soldier bee that had just been relieved from securing the perimeter. Dex stopped the soldier bee to talk to him.

"Can I ask you a question?" asked Dex. "Sure," replied the soldier bee.

"Why is it that bees have never spoken to humans?"

"I don't know, but that's the rule," replied the soldier bee, and he walked on.

Dex was irritated by the soldier bee's answer. That boy had spoken to him, so why shouldn't he speak back to the boy? Dex made up his mind. He was going to find the boy, follow him home, and speak to him. Dex knew that in order to find the boy, he was going to have to go back to the playground, which meant another possible encounter with that garden spider.

Dex knew no other bees—not even the queen—would be looking for him since he had the day off. Only forager bees were allowed to venture well beyond the hive's perimeter because of their experience dealing with the outside world. The queen, for accountability purposes, had to be notified about any bee that planned to leave. Dex decided not to tell the queen because he feared she would deny his request.

Dex took off for the playground. He knew it was too early to meet the boy on his route, so he decided to forage for nectar and pollen, just to pass the time. When the time drew close for the boy's arrival, Dex flew to the playground. When Dex got close to the bushes, he flew high over them and then he lowered himself just above them. Once he established a safe distance from the bushes, he watched for the boy.

While Dex was waiting, he took notice of the spot on the

ground where he had been unwrapped from the web by the boy.

"That's the very spot where the boy saved me," Dex said to himself. He sighed and smiled. He really thought, in his heart, that he was doing the right thing.

Suddenly, his quiet thoughts were interrupted by a voice talking to him.

"You know, I caught a beetle this morning," said the voice. "It tasted salty, as usual."

Dex turned around and looked down. Sitting just below him was the garden spider. The spider had rebuilt his web in the same exact spot, on top of the bushes.

Although Dex was hovering a safe distance from the spider, he flew a little bit further away just to be safer.

"What are you doing here?" Dex asked.

"I live here, Bee," snapped the spider. "I should be asking you that question."

"It's none of your business why I'm here," replied Dex. "What do you care anyway? You tried to eat me."

The spider, clearly annoyed, shook his head. "*Drink!* I tried to *drink* you. It doesn't matter anyway, because that . . . boy ruined my dinner and dessert. I had a succulent butterfly dinner that could have been followed by delicious honeybee dessert." The spider pointed at Dex. "That meddling boy and that stick ruined the best meal I would've ever had!"

"You're sick!" yelled Dex.

"I'm a spider! It's what I do," the spider retorted. "At least I don't go around robbing flowers of their nectar and pollen just to make that nasty fluid you guys call honey!" The spider walked out until he was in the middle of his web. "I sure wish a gust of wind would blow you into my web right now!" said the spider. "I've grown tired of these subpar insects. I need something . . . tastier."

While the spider was talking, Dex turned around and

saw the boy walking a short distance away. Dex became excited and turned back to the spider. "Sorry, Spider. I hate to "wrap" this conversation up, but I have to go." Dex flew away to get in position to follow the boy.

"Buzz off, bee," said the spider, and he retreated into the bushes.

Dex didn't want the boy to see him yet, so he flew upward. The boy walked past Dex and didn't see him. Dex waited a few seconds and began to follow the boy home. He looked around as he followed him. He had never been this far from the hive. He took mental pictures so he could remember his way back.

The boy walked about two blocks farther from the bush before he stopped and opened the gate to his house.

"He's home," whispered Dex.

Dex watched as the boy felt his front pockets and then his back pockets. He was looking for his house keys. The boy put down his backpack and began an all-out search for them.

While the boy looked for his keys, Dex dove down and landed on his backpack. He nestled himself under the pocket flap so he wouldn't be seen. Finally, the boy found his keys. He picked up his backpack, opened the door, and walked in—with Dex in tow.

"Hi, Mom. I'm home," said Max. He went into the kitchen where his mother was and gave her a hug.

"Hey Max," said Mrs. Thomas. "How was school?"

"Better than yesterday," Max said, with a smile. He went to the fridge to grab an apple.

"Wash your hands!" exclaimed Mrs. Thomas.

Max stopped in his tracks, washed his hands, and then went back to the fridge to get the apple. "I'm about to go to my room and get started on my homework, Mom," said Max as he was leaving the kitchen.

"Okay. Dinner will be ready in about an hour," said Mrs. Thomas.

Max picked up his backpack and ran upstairs to his room. When he got to his room, he placed his apple on the desk and dropped his backpack on the floor. He then grabbed the apple and began to eat it.

While Max was eating his apple, Dex climbed out of the backpack and quickly hid under Max's bed. Max finished his apple and tossed the core into his wastebasket. He then took out his books, jumped onto the bed, and started on his homework.

Dex, still under Max's bed, started to get nervous. He wondered how the boy would react. Would he panic? Would he swat at him? Would he try to trap him and put him in a jar?

Dex found himself lost in these thoughts and got scared. He quickly shook himself out of those thoughts, regained his bravery, and began to focus.

He noticed that the window across the room was open. There was also a desk next to the window. Dex figured that he would speak to the boy from the desk. That way, if he attempted to swat at him or try to trap him, he would have a way to escape.

Dex walked out from under the bed and slowly climbed up the wall. He looked over to see if the coast was clear. When he saw that it was, he flew the rest of the way to the desk. Once Dex made it to the desk, he suddenly felt more confident. He took a deep breath. "Here goes," he said to himself, and he finally spoke: "Hi there, human!"

Max rose up, turned, and looked both ways. Seeing nothing, he dismissed the voice. "Eh, I guess it came from outside," he said.

"No, it didn't," said Dex.

Max quickly jumped out of his bed. "Who said that?" he asked. Max was looking in Dex's direction, but he didn't see where the voice was coming from.

"I'm on your desk, by the window," said Dex.

Max slowly walked toward the desk.

Dex grew nervous, and he started to walk backward to the window.

"Did you just speak to me, Bee?" asked Max as he picked up one of his shoes.

"Yes, I did," replied Dex. "Please put down the shoe. I'm not going to sting you."

"Why are you in my room?" asked Max. "And how are you talking to me?" Max rubbed his hands through his hair in disbelief.

"You saved my life yesterday," Dex explained. "I wanted to thank you."

"You're the bee I saved yesterday?"

"Yes."

Max quickly ran over to his door and closed it. "My mom and my sister hate insects. If either one of them sees you, let alone hears you talking, they're going to freak out."

"Does that mean you are going to put down that shoe?" asked Dex.

Max looked down, realized he was still holding onto his shoe, and quickly dropped it. He walked over, kneeled down and looked intently at Dex.

Dex, sensing that the boy was not going to harm him, walked over toward him.

"What is your name?" Max asked.

"My name is Dex. What is your name?"

"My name is Max."

"It is truly a pleasure to meet you, Max."

Max extended his finger out to Dex. Dex stared at the finger with a perplexed look on his face. "What are you doing?" he asked.

"Handshake," Max explained. He then took both of his hands and grasped them, as if to handshake with himself. "It's what we do when we meet each other for the first time or when we greet each other." Max extended his finger out to Dex again. "I just met you for the first time, so shake my hand . . . err . . . finger, since you're so small."

Dex walked over and put his front leg onto Max's finger. Max then moved his finger up and down. "There—now we have officially met," Max laughed. "I still can't believe that I am talking to an actual bee!"

"I still can't believe I'm talking to a real live human!" Dex answered excitedly. He then realized he had to get back to the hive. He really wanted to stay and talk more with Max, but it was time to go. "I'm afraid I have to go, Max."

"Will you come back to visit?"

"I don't know. Leave your window open during the day, and I might stop by."

"Okay," Max agreed.

Dex smiled at his new friend, then spread his wings and flew to the windowsill. He looked back at Max. "Thank you so much for saving my life, Max."

"You're welcome, Dex," said Max.

As Dex flew out the window, Max sat in disbelief at what just happened. He smiled, shook his head, and went back to his bed to finish his homework.

# CHAPTER SIX

## A BUDDING FRIENDSHIP

Dex was excited that he had a human friend. He flew up as high as he could, and then he torpedoed back down. He flew as if he didn't have a care in the world. He then landed on the same windowsill from the previous day, and he practiced his handshake. "It's weird but I like it," he commented to himself.

Dex thought about his decision not to tell the queen about leaving the hive for the day. He figured she was aware that he had left the hive without her permission by now. "Well, time to face the music," he said to himself, and he headed for home.

When Dex arrived at the hive, a guard bee met him. "The queen has requested your presence, Dex," the guard bee sneered.

"I know, I know."

The guard bee escorted Dex to the queen's throne room.

"Dex, have you not grown tired of being in my throne room? Where did you go today without notifying me?"

The queen was upset, Dex could tell. He swallowed hard and answered, "I went to visit the boy who saved me."

All the bees in the queen's throne room began speaking

among themselves in disbelief until the queen quickly stood up, left her throne, and flew toward Dex. "Leave us!" she ordered the other bees.

The room cleared out leaving the queen and Dex alone. "Did you get pollen on your brain, Dex?" the queen blurted. "Are you trying to get yourself killed?"

"I just wanted to thank the boy for saving my life, Your Majesty," Dex began.

"And how were you going to do that?" the queen spit out. "We don't talk to humans!" She paused and looked at Dex carefully. "You spoke to that human, didn't you?"

"I did," Dex admitted. "Actual words! And he wants me to come back to visit."

The queen sighed and flew back to her throne and faced Dex. "We do not speak to humans!" she shouted.

"Why not?" asked Dex.

The queen thought for a minute, and then spoke. "I don't know why not, but that is the rule."

Dex shook his head in disbelief at her answer and the queen shook her head in disappointment. "You obviously feel very strongly about this, Dex, and I am really trying to understand this whole thing, but the fact of the matter is we do not trust humans."

"I trust this one, Your Majesty."

The queen sighed. "You only met him twice! What am I going to do with you, Dex? I could have you detained, but what will that solve? You are still going to visit the human anyway after I let you go. You have your mind made up." The queen knew her bees very well and she could tell Dex felt strongly about this human.

She then reluctantly softened her stance and spoke again. "Dex, if you feel this strongly about this human, I will let you visit him—but you are on your own. If something happens to you while you are with the human, your distress buzz will be ignored. You will continue to fulfill your foraging duties with Tank first. After you are done, you are free to visit the human. Am I clear, Dex?"

Dex nodded in agreement. "Yes, Your Majesty."

"Then you are dismissed."

Dex acknowledged the queen and turned to leave when she called back to him. "Dex," she said, fighting back tears. "Please be careful out there, okay? The humans are so unpredictable."

Dex walked back to the throne and hugged the queen. "I will, Your Majesty. I truly believe something good will come out of all of this."

***

Max finished his homework and went downstairs to eat. He was still thinking about Dex and the brief conversation they'd had together. He really hoped that Dex would come back tomorrow to visit after school. Max wanted to tell somebody else about his encounter, but he thought it would be better not to bring that kind of attention to him or Dex. Probably no one would believe him anyway.

His mother looked over at Max and saw him in deep thought. "Max, is everything okay?" she asked.

"Yeah, Mom—I'm okay," he replied. "I have a big day tomorrow at school so I'm going to bed early tonight."

A confused look came over Mrs. Thomas's face but she shrugged her shoulders. "Okay."

Max really wanted to go to bed early so the next day could arrive faster and he could talk to Dex again. Suddenly, an idea popped into Max's head that sparked his enthusiasm. He asked his mom if he could be excused from the dinner table and once excused, Max jumped up to go outside.

“Be right back, Mom,” he called out. Max wanted to see if any other insects would speak to him. He came across an anthill in his lawn, so he kneeled down to speak.

“Hi, ants. Can you any of you speak to me?” he asked.

There was no answer from the ants, as they scattered back to safety in the anthill.

Max walked farther down his block, and he saw a beetle resting on a branch. "Hey, beetle. Can you talk back to me, please?" The beetle walked along without saying a word to him. Then Max thought about that garden spider that he'd rescued Dex from. "Hmm, maybe that spider will talk to me," he said to himself. He hopped on his bike and rode over to the bushes where the spider was sitting.

"Hey, spider," Max spoke excitedly. "Come out and talk to me!"

The garden spider crawled out, took one look at Max, and jumped out of his web, scurrying under the bushes and out of the boy's sight.

Max walked home feeling discouraged. He knew only one insect was going to speak to him, and he would have to wait until tomorrow. Even then, it wasn't guaranteed that Dex was coming back.

The next day at school, Max could not wait until the end of the day so he could rush back home to possibly meet up with Dex.

Dex was out foraging with Tank in the neighborhood that same day and he could not wait to finish so he could go over to Max's house.

Finally, after what seemed like an eternity, Max was out of school and he was on his way home.

Dex was emptying his pollen and nectar at the hive, and when he was finished, he quickly flew out the hive, flying straight to Max's house.

When Max arrived home, he quickly washed his hands, grabbed an apple from the fridge and rushed upstairs to his room. He opened his window and sat at his desk, waiting for Dex to show up.

"I sure hope he comes today," Max said to himself. He finished eating his apple and tossed the core into his waste basket. Twenty minutes went by, and Max grew restless. "He's probably not coming today," he said sadly.

Dex arrived a few minutes later and found Max with his head buried in his arms at his desk. "Hi, Max. Did I come at a bad time?" he asked.

Max sat up quickly. "No, not at all!" He then quickly closed his bedroom door. "I didn't think you would show up."

"I wanted to show up today," said Dex.

"I have many questions to ask you," Max told Dex excitedly.

"You do? Ok . . . let's hear them."

"First question: how you are able to speak?" asked Max.

"We always have been able to speak; we just don't speak to humans."

"Why not?"

Dex shrugged. "I don't know. I guess it's some kind of rule."

"Why did you speak to me then?" asked Max.

"I wanted to tell you thanks for saving my life, and I wanted you to hear me say it, I guess," Dex remarked.

"Wow," said Max in amazement.

"Bees don't trust humans," said Dex.

"I can see why they don't," Max agreed. "People normally kill insects—especially when they get into our homes. My mom and sister really hate insects."

"Why?"

"Because they're girls," Max replied, as if that explained everything.

"Our queen told us to never go near humans," Dex continued. "They destroyed our last home, but I was just a larva so I don't remember it."

"What's a larva?" Max wondered.

"It's a baby bee," answered Dex.

"Oh, we just say baby."

"Fascinating," marveled Dex.

"I wasn't too fond of bees myself, because you guys sting a lot," Max admitted.

"We only sting in self-defense and to protect our hive." "Do bees die after you sting?"

"We have three levels on our stings," Dex explained. "The first is our defensive sting to fight off a predator that tries to eat us or to ward off humans. The second level to our stings inflicts more pain, and our stinger goes in deeper, leaving a nasty wound and swelling. The final level is the sacrificial sting. We bury our stinger deep into the skin and we leave it in. We cannot pull our stinger out once we use our sacrificial sting because our stinger is a part of our abdomen. This is our last resort, and we only use this to defend our hive."

"Wow, that's deep," Max nodded in admiration. "Okay, next question: how do bees make honey?"

"Well, it's really not that hard but I'll explain it to you," said Dex. "First, we collect the pollen and nectar from the flowers in the neighborhood. Then we store the nectar in our stomachs."

"Your stomachs?" asked Max incredulously. "Ugh, disgusting!"

"Yeah, we have two stomachs: one for storing and one for digesting."

"You have two stomachs?" asked Max.

"Yeah, you don't?"

"Nope. Just one, and storing nectar in your stomach just sounds disgusting," Max declared.

"You got a better place for me to store it?" Dex challenged good-naturedly.

"Yeah. In a pail or a bucket," Max suggested.

"Yeah—a bunch of bees flying around with pails and buckets collecting nectar and pollen," Dex said sarcastically. "What could be more ridiculous than that?"

"Hmm, how about a bee that's talking to me in my room?" Max responded mockingly.

"I guess you are right, Max," Dex laughed. "Okay. Let me finish. After we collect the nectar 'in our stomachs,' we fly back to the hive to empty the pollen from our sacks on our legs, and we empty the nectar from our stomachs through our mouths."

Max listened attentively while Dex spoke. He was still in awe that an actual bee was talking to him.

"Then the bees at the hive gather around and transfer the nectar from mouth to mouth until most of the moisture is gone."

Max grew sick as he listened to this. "Mouth to mouth?" he asked.

"Yes. That's how we make our honey," replied Dex.

"After that, we store it in our cells and seal it with beeswax."

"What about the pollen?" asked Max.

"Oh, we mix the pollen with some of the nectar and we make bee bread to feed the larvae."

"So, that jar of honey in our kitchen downstairs is basically bee's vomit?" asked Max.

"I guess it is," Dex replied. "What is vomit?"

"Sometimes when humans eat food that is bad, we throw it up, which is called vomit." Max thought for a minute and then looked at Dex. "Well," he said, laughing. "I guess honey is the best vomit I have ever tasted."

"Thanks, I'm glad you approve." Dex began laughing as well. "Do you have any friends?" he asked Max.

"Not really," Max shrugged. "I hang out with a few of the kids at school, but that's it. I don't have any friends that come over."

"Why not?"

"I don't know. It's not like I don't want to have friends come over; it just didn't happen yet, I guess."

"If you say so," said Dex. "No pressure from me to make you find friends." He flew over to the window. "I have to go now, Max. I'm so glad I met you."

"Me too," said Max. "Be careful out there."

"I will." Dex flew home.

# CHAPTER SEVEN

## TRAITOR VS. LOYALTY

The next day, Dex and Tank went out foraging, and Tank hardly spoke a word to Dex while they were out. Dex could tell that Tank did not like that he could go over to Max's house to talk and also thought that Tank was a bit jealous of the time he was going to spend with Max and not Tank. Dex figured it would be best to talk with Tank on their next break to clear the growing tension between the two friends.

"Tank, why are you so quiet?" Dex asked.

"I really don't like that you are talking to that human," Tank told him. "You know they can't be trusted, Dex. I don't understand why the queen would even let you go over to the human's house in the first place."

"Are you jealous, Tank?" Dex asked with a smile.

Tank laughed. "Of course not. Why would I be? He only has two legs; I have six."

Dex laughed. "I know this bothers you a lot, Tank, but trust me—this will never get between our friendship. We will always be the Zoom and Boom Connection."

"I know," Tank admitted. "I also know if that boy wanted to harm you, he would have done it already. However, I must be honest with you, Dex. I don't like this one bit. The other bees are talking and most of them have labeled you as a traitor."

"What do *you* think, Tank? Am I a traitor?"

"I don't think you're a traitor, but you have to admit that this isn't a good look for you right now," replied Tank.

"I know it isn't, but something inside me makes me think that something really good is going to come out of all of this," Dex argued.

Tank sighed and shook his head. "Dex, we are friends and will always stay friends. However, my loyalty is with the hive. I didn't want you to put me in a position where I would have to choose. The welfare of the entire hive is important."

Dex looked at his friend and nodded. "I understand, Tank."

"You can still just forget that human and let things get back to normal, Dex," Tank suggested.

"Not gonna happen," Dex replied.

"It was worth a shot to ask," Tank shrugged.

Dex smiled at Tank and they finished up and headed back to the hive.

***

When they were finished emptying their pollen and nectar, one of the worker bees spoke to Tank.

“Hi, Tank. How did the foraging go today?” the worker bee asked.

“Pretty good foraging,” replied Tank. “Lots of nectar was brought back today.”

The other bee then looked at Dex. “If you are done here, you can go,” he snapped.

Dex wanted to say something back to the bee, but he thought better of it and left.

Tank followed behind him. “You’re going back to the human’s house?” he asked.

"Yeah," replied Dex. "I'll be back later. You want to hang out tonight?"

"Nah, I'm turning in early tonight. Maybe we can hang out another night."

"Okay. See you." Just as Dex was flying away, he heard one of the guard bees call him a traitor. He looked back and the guard bee was shaking his head.

***

Dex had a lot on his mind as he flew to Max's house. He knew Tank was not going to bed early; Tank just didn't want to hang out with him. He was also sad that the hive was turning against him. Dex really felt that something positive was going to come out of all of this—he just didn't know what it was yet. He was, however, determined more than ever to prove it to the other bees.

Dex arrived at Max's house and entered through the window. Max was not in his room yet, so Dex decided to wait until he came back. While he waited, he began looking around Max's room. He flew around looking at the strange pictures the human had hanging on his walls. He flew over Max's bed and studied the strange designs on his blanket. He flew back to the window and started crawling on it. He liked the way the glass felt on his feet. "This glass is so cold on my feet," he said.

***

Joanna walked past Max's room and noticed a bee

crawling on the window. Dex, still fascinated by the coolness of the glass, did not see Joanna watching him. She quickly ran downstairs to get the bug spray. "Ugh, I hate bugs!" she cried in disgust. She ran back upstairs and peeked around the doorway to see if the bee was still there. When she saw that he was, she began to tiptoe closer to him.

Dex was too busy pressing his face against the window to notice Joanna creeping slowly toward him with a spray can of bug killer aimed at him.

Max came up the stairs from outside and saw Joanna in his room. "What are you doing in my room, Joanna?!"

Joanna didn't turn around, but Dex did just as she started to spray him. The mist covered Dex as he flew out the window. He landed on the siding of the house, coughing and rubbing his eyes.

Joanna turned and frowned at Max. "You let that bee get away, moron!" she yelled.

Max raced to the window, looking for Dex. Then he turned around and looked at Joanna. "Get out of my room!" he screamed.

Joanna ran out of the room. "I'm telling Mom you yelled at me!" she cried as she ran downstairs.

Max closed the door and ran back to the window. "Dex, where are you?" he called. "Are you okay? She's gone now; she's not coming back."

Dex flew back in slowly, still rubbing his eyes. "I'm fine. What did she spray on me?"

"Bug spray," Max answered. "It kills all insects, including bees. I told you they really hate insects. I left the house for a minute, and I forgot to close the window. I'm sorry, Dex."

"It's okay, Max. You saved my life again."

Max smiled and sat down on his bed while Dex rested on the desk. "This has not been a good day for me," Dex confided. "My hive is upset with me because I'm hanging out with you."

"Really?"

"Yeah—they're calling me a traitor."

"Wow!" Max shook his head sadly. "Are they going to kick you out?"

"I don't think so. Only the queen can do something like that, not the hive."

"I hope you don't get kicked out—but, if you ever do, you can stay with me," Max offered.

"Thanks," said Dex. "Just make sure you are in the room next time."

"Okay, when the window is up, come in. When the window is closed, obviously you can't come in," Max chuckled.

"Sounds good to me," Dex agreed. "I've had enough drama for one day. It's time for me to go."

"Okay, I'll see you tomorrow, Dex. Get some rest, and we will try this again . . . without the bug spray," Max added, laughing.

"Very funny, Max. I'll see you tomorrow." Dex then opened up his wings and flew out the window.

Max closed the window and joined his family downstairs.

# CHAPTER EIGHT

## THE BAN

A few weeks went by, and Max and Dex grew closer in their friendship. Dex learned that Max loved to eat pizza, his favorite dessert was vanilla ice cream, and he loved to watch baseball, football, and basketball on TV.

Max learned that Dex loved to fly fast, he loved to drink flower nectar early in the morning, and he detested spiders. In the beginning, Dex used to stay a few minutes, now he stayed about an hour.

Max's parents had started to notice his unusual behavior, and they were wondering how to approach him. At the hive, the queen was aware of how her bees felt about Dex, and how they thought he was a traitor. There were some bees that sided with Dex; however, the majority was not on his side and that caused some division —exactly what the queen was trying to keep out of her hive.

One day after school, Max and Dex were hanging out in Max's room, Dex resting on Max's pillow.

"Dex, can I see what your hive looks like?" Max asked.

Dex thought about it for a minute and answered, "I guess you can, but you can't go too close. If the bees see you, they will attack you, and it will be a long run for you."

"I'll be on my bike, Dex," Max insisted.

"Bike, on foot, or car—bees will chase you for up to about 300 yards," Dex explained with a smile.

*"300 yards?"* asked Max. "That's three football fields! Okay, I won't go close to it. I'll get my dad's binoculars and we can go."

"I'll meet you outside." Dex quickly flew out the window while Max grabbed the binoculars and raced down the stairs. He saw his mom and dad sitting in the living room.

"Max, come here for a second," Mr. Thomas called. "What's going on with the weird behavior lately, Son?"

"Uh . . . how am I acting weird, Dad?" Max wondered.

"You don't go outside as much as you used to. You stay in your room way too much now, and Joanna said she's heard you talking to yourself while you are in your room," Mrs. Thomas explained.

"Mom, Dad, everything is fine," Max assured them with a smile. "I've been bored going outside lately, and I've been thinking out loud in my room, that's all. Can I go outside now?"

"*Now* you want to go outside?" Mr. Thomas shook his head. "You just said you were bored going outside, Son."

"I know, but now I want to go," Max insisted.

"Fine. Go ahead, but be back by dinner."

Max raced outside to meet up with Dex; Mr. Thomas looked at his wife and smiled; "Kids," he said.

***

Max put on his helmet, hopped on his bike, and looked at Dex. "Ever been on a bike ride before?" he asked. Dex shook his head. "You can sit on my helmet and tell me how to get to your hive while I ride," said Max.

Dex could not wait to see how fast Max could go on his bike. He flew up, landed on Max's helmet, and gripped tightly so he wouldn't fall off.

"Hold on, Dex," Max ordered, and he began to pedal, soon at top speed.

Dex closed his eyes and felt the wind blow across his face. He'd never flown this fast in his life. He spread out his wings to pretend he was flying that fast. "This is so cool!" Dex yelled.

Soon, Dex was yelling out directions on how to get to his hive, and ten minutes later they arrived at his home. The field was enormous with small trees spread about. The grass was very tall, reaching up to Max's waist, and was yellow and dried out from a lack of water. There was a FOR SALE sign hidden by the grass.

"Where is the hive?" Max asked as he pulled out his binoculars.

"It's in the tree in the middle of the field."

Max pulled his binoculars to his eyes. "Wow, I see it!" he said excitedly. "I wish I could get a closer look."

"This is as close as you can go," Dex ordered sternly. "The

last thing we need is an angry swarm chasing you."

"How long have you lived over here?" asked Max.

"Just about my entire life," Dex replied. "I was a larva when we moved here." He looked around to make sure no other bees were in sight. "Okay, Max. You saw the hive. It's time for you to go before you are spotted."

"Okay. I'll see you tomorrow, Dex." Max pedaled away, heading home. Once Dex saw Max turn the corner, he headed to the hive.

***

Dex was in his quarters when two guard bees barged in, seized him by the wings, and flew him to the queen's throne.

Tank was there, and he looked angry.

"Dex, I am going to ask you one time," the queen said sternly. "Did you bring the human to our home?"

Dex looked at Tank and scowled. He figured Tank had seen him with Max and had informed the queen. "Yes, Your Majesty, I did," Dex admitted as he hung his head.

"I guess it wasn't enough that I let you go visit the human daily? You had to go and bring him to our *home?* Now the human knows where we live! This has gone far enough, Dex! I never thought I would ever do this during my tenure as queen." She stood up, and with a stern look in her eyes, she took a deep breath and spoke slowly. "As queen of this hive, and with all who are here as witnesses, I declare that the welfare of this hive has just been threatened by this negligent act by Dex. Therefore, I hereby ban Dex from this hive effective immediately! Guards, escort Dex from the hive!"

Tank's face dropped in surprise. He had thought that Dex would only be detained for a while, not banned. Dex teared up as he was escorted out of the throne room. He dejectedly looked back at Tank. "Does this make you happy?" he yelled.

Tank could not even look at Dex. He was feeling just as bad himself, and he felt guilty for betraying his best friend.

The guard bees took Dex to the hive opening and tossed him out. "Do yourself and the hive a favor and get stuck in that spider's web again," said one of the guard bees. "And don't escape this time!" Both guard bees laughed and went back into the hive.

Dex was left alone outside and it was becoming dark. He had nowhere else to go but then remembered Max telling him that if he was ever kicked out of the hive, he could stay with him. Dex flew towards Max's house and arrived just as it was getting darker. He was relieved to find Max in his room watching TV. Dex tapped on the window to get Max's attention.

Max looked over and saw Dex outside, so he opened the window to let him in. Dex explained everything to Max.

"I'm so sorry I got you kicked out of your hive, Dex," Max said. "This is all my fault."

"It's not your fault Max. The hive is afraid of you because they don't know or understand who you are. Not every human is bad; just like every insect is not out to bite or sting people. I just need to give them some time and eventually they will come around. I don't know when, but I'm willing to go through this until they do. If they don't, then at least I gave this an honest try."

"Well, until they come around, you can stay here with me," said Max. "You're going to need somewhere to sleep. I'll be right back."

Max left the room and closed the door, and soon returned holding a small, black, suede ring box. He opened the box and stuffed four cotton balls into it.

“What is that?” Dex asked.

“It’s your new bed,” Max told him. “Try it out. See if you like it.”

Dex crawled into the ring box. “It’s so soft,” he said. “I love it!”

Max set the ring box on the shelf on the wall next to his bed.

“My entire bee family—whom I have known all my life—have turned their backs on me after a few weeks. You have welcomed me like a friend since day one. I am grateful to have you as a friend, Max. I will never forget this.”

“Everything will turn out to be fine, Dex. I believe it.”

“Time for bed, Max,” Mr. Thomas called from downstairs. Max turned off his TV and went to the bathroom to brush his teeth. Dex followed him in.

"What are you doing?"

"I'm about to brush my teeth," Max replied, and he showed Dex his teeth. "Do you have any teeth?"

"No," Dex said.

"Well, you can watch me brush mine."

"Okay." Dex landed on the sink to watch. He looked on as Max's mouth foamed up as he brushed his teeth. Max then spit out the foamy toothpaste and swished with water, finally brushing his tongue. He rinsed with water again, and then he finished with a rinse with mouthwash. When Max was done, he looked at Dex and flashed a big toothy grin. "Aaaahhhh!!! All clean!"

"Disgusting," said Dex.

He and Max laughed. They both went to their beds, talked quietly for a little while, and soon, both friends were fast asleep.

# CHAPTER NINE

## THE FARM

Several weeks passed by and it was now late May. The weather was slowly transitioning from spring to summer. All the kids were still in school, but they were counting down the days until summer vacation.

Dex, still banned from the hive, missed his friends terribly. He missed his foraging adventures with Tank and the closeness all the bees had with one another. He was definitely "hive sick."

Max loved that Dex was living with him, as he had a best friend in Dex, but he knew Dex missed his hive. Max wondered how he could lift his friend's spirits.

While Max was at school one day, he learned he was going on a field trip to a farm. "I should take Dex with me," Max said to himself. "Maybe that will cheer him up a bit." He could not wait to get home and tell Dex the news. When he arrived at his house, he went to his room and found Dex looking out the window.

"Hi, Dex," Max greeted excitedly. "Guess what? I'm going on a field trip tomorrow!"

"That's nice," Dex mumbled. "Where are you going?"

"We're going to a farm that is not too far from my grandparents' house, and I'm taking you with me!"

Dex turned around and looked at Max. "You want me to go with you?" he asked.

"Yes," Max replied. "You need to get away and see something different. I know you've had a rough time and you miss your hive but sitting around here moping is not going to help things."

Dex gave some serious thought to what Max had said and then agreed. "I guess you're right. Ok . . . I'll go with you."

***

The next morning, Max jumped out of bed as soon as the alarm went off. He loved to go on field trips. He always went to bed extra early the night before a field trip so he could get up early to prepare his lunch and make sure he wouldn't forget anything.

Dex was already awake and outside collecting some nectar and pollen for the trip. Max waited until Dex came back from outside, and when he returned, he climbed under Max's collar to keep from being seen.

Once Dex was secure, Max hurried to the kitchen to eat breakfast, and then he was off to school. At school, Max's teacher conducted a head count, and they all got on the school bus. Soon, they were off to the farm.

Max sat in the middle of the bus. It was not clear for Dex to come out, so Dex dug his legs into the fibers of Max's shirt so he wouldn't fall out. There, he took a quick nap.

After a short time, the bus arrived at the farm and the kids got off the bus.

The farm was huge. It looked like it went on for miles. There was a big red barn that some of the animals lived in and cows grazed on grass behind the barn. Chickens ran unbothered in and out the barn while pigs basked in the sun in their mud pit.

There was so much to do on the farm. The class climbed on a huge tractor that was no longer in use. Each kid took turns sitting in the driver's seat to make believe they were driving it. The other kids played on the giant wheels waiting their turn to sit in the driver's seat. Max was very careful while he played, as he didn't want to injure Dex, who was still under his collar. Some of the activities Max skipped altogether, just to be safe.

Later, the kids went to milk a few of the cows but Max thought that was disgusting. He didn't like the feel of the cow's udder as he milked it. The class then fed goats, pigs, and horses and picked some of the crops that the farmers grew. The farm even had a few tire swings set up for the kids to play on. Soon, it was time for the class to eat lunch, and everyone sat outside near one of the smaller barns.

While Max was eating, Dex decided to fill up his nectar supply. He wanted to sample some of the flavors from the different crops they did not have in his neighborhood. First, he went to the apple tree and sipped some nectar from the tree's flowers. "Mmmm, tangy and sweet," Dex said. Then he flew over to the orange tree and sipped from its flowers. "Refreshing—almost like I should be drinking this nectar in the morning!" He then flew over to the lemon tree and sipped on its nectar, and his eyes widened with delight. This nectar had the perfect blend of sweetness, and it had a strong citrusy flavor that Dex could not resist. "This lemon nectar and pollen tastes far better than the dandelion nectar and pollen I've collected!" Dex said in excitement. He then filled his second stomach with all the lemon nectar.

By the time lunch was over, Dex had sampled different types of nectar and pollen from over twenty different crops and trees. Dex was in nectar heaven. He could barely hold himself up as he flew back to meet with Max because he was so full.

When Dex returned to Max, Max was listening to his teacher speak about the next part of the tour. Dex made sure no other kids were looking, and when all was clear, he landed on Max's shoulder and crawled under his collar. "This place is amazing, Max!" he whispered excitedly.

Max slightly nodded his head. "I know," he replied, talking out the side of his mouth. "We're about to go see the beekeeper."

"A beekeeper?" Dex repeated.

"Yeah, you'll see."

"Max, who are you talking to?" his teacher asked suddenly.

"Um, nobody."

"Then stop talking when I'm talking." Some of the kids laughed then.

"Dex, stop talking to me before I get in trouble," Max mumbled.

"Sorry, Max," Dex replied, holding back his chuckle.

***

Dex stayed under Max's collar as the class made their way to the beekeeper. Dex wanted to know what a beekeeper was and why they keep bees.

The students entered a massive building and were led to a room with a large window. The window looked into a room where all of the bees were housed, and the kids were able to watch without being stung. Several boxes were lined up together.

"Where are the hives?" asked Max.

"The hives are in the boxes," the teacher replied. "It's called an apiary."

Dex slowly peeked out from Max's collar to take a closer look. This hive looked nothing like his hive; these hives here were man-made, but Dex's hive was made naturally.

A man walked into the room to tend to the boxes. "That is a beekeeper or *apiarist.* He takes care of the bees," the teacher explained.

Dex's jaw dropped. The beekeeper was a human! Dex wanted to take a closer look at the beekeeper and see the human-made hive. "I'll be right back," he whispered to Max. "I'll meet you at the bus when it's time to go."

Max gave a slight nod, and Dex snuck out of the building to see the hives. He also got a closer look at the beekeeper.

The beekeeper was dressed in a white, baggy suit and wore a large, brimmed hat on his head that had a net surrounding his face. He also wore big white gloves. He was dressed to protect himself from potential bee stings.

The apiarist took the top off one of the boxes and sprayed smoke into it, then he pulled out one of the frames. The frame was covered in honey and beeswax. Some bees came out, but they did not attack the beekeeper. In fact, it looked like the bees were letting him take some honey.

As Dex was watching this, one of the bees from the hive approached him. "You're not from around here, are you?" he asked.

"Nope," Dex replied.

"Where are my manners?" the bee asked. "My name is Trint."

Dex introduced himself and then extended one of his legs out to Trint.

"What is that?" asked Trint.

"Handshake," replied Dex.

"But we don't have any hands," said Trint with a confused look.

"Just try it."

Trint shrugged and slowly extended his front leg. Dex gripped Trint's leg and shook it. "It's a pleasure to meet you, Trint."

"You're from the city, huh?" asked Trint.

"Suburbs."

"Never been there."

"Does that human . . . keep you?" asked Dex.

"Yeah, he's our keeper," Trint told him. "They provided us with a home when we outgrew our old hive. We traveled for a few days before we found this place."

"Why did he use that smoke on your hive?" Dex wondered.

"Oh, that smoke is harmless. That's just to let us know that he's coming to get some honey and to check on us to see if we are okay."

"Do you talk to him?" asked Dex.

"No," said Trint sharply. "Why would we do that?"

"Oh, nothing; just asking," Dex replied nervously. He looked around and admired the scenery. "Looks like these bees have it made living here."

"Yeah, we all work together with the humans. We work for them, and they work for us. We work to provide for humans and animals together. The humans provide all those trees, crops, and flowers for us to collect our nectar. We pollinate those flowers so they can produce fruits and vegetables. The humans and animals eat the fruits and vegetables that the plants produce. We also give the humans some of our honey in return."

"Pollinate?" asked Dex. "What's that?"

"You don't know what pollinating is?" asked Trint

incredulously. "You only pollinate every single day when you're out foraging. I'm assuming you are a forager, right?"

"Yeah," replied Dex.

"Come with me, Dex," said Trint with a smile on his face. "Looks like I have to teach you some things to take back to your hive in the suburbs."

Trint led Dex to the apple tree, and they landed in one of the flowers. "This is called a stamen," he explained. "This is where bees collect our pollen. Most of the time, after we leave a flower, we're covered in pollen." Trint pointed to his face to show Dex the pollen that was stuck on his body. "Then we go to another flower." He then flew to a flower a few inches away. "Now, as I'm collecting nectar from this flower, the pollen from the other flower will be transferred to the stigma in this flower. This flower is fertilized and will later produce apples."

Dex thought about the flowers he collected nectar and pollen from. "Wow!" he exclaimed.

"We're pollinators, Dex. Without bees, many of the foods humans and animals eat would die off forever. So, we're kind of a big deal in this world."

"My hive does not trust humans," Dex admitted. "They avoid them as much as possible."

"Tell me something, Dex. When you go out every morning to forage in your neighborhood, where do you go?"

Dex thought about it for a moment, and then he

answered: "The humans' front and back yards."

"Exactly!" exclaimed Trint. "You need the humans to plant the flowers; the flowers need you to pollinate them; you need the nectar and pollen from the flowers to make honey; and the flowers produce food for the animals and humans after you pollinate them—assuming they have a garden. I understand, Dex, that not all humans are friendly toward us. But there are many humans, like the ones on this farm, who appreciate us and what we can do."

Trint turned around toward the open field where the crops were, and he pointed. "This is for all of us," he said. "Humans and bees work together in perfect harmony to do our part to help provide food for everyone. Isn't it beautiful, Dex?"

"Yes, it is, my friend."

"Follow me. I have something for you." Trint led Dex to his hive. Dex waited at the front opening while Trint went inside. When he came back, he gave Dex some honey and some beebread. "Take this for your trip back to the suburbs," he said.

Dex tasted some of the beebread and the honey, and he closed his eyes and shook his head in disbelief. "This is the best honey and beebread I have ever tasted. I can taste all the flavors of the nectar and pollen I sampled earlier. I wish my hive could live here."

"This place welcomes all bees," Trint offered.

Dex looked back and saw the kids lining up to get honey samples at the school bus and he knew it was time to go.

"Thank you, Trint, for showing me what our true purpose is as bees. I hope to see you again sometime."

"You know where to find me now," Trint said with a smile on his face. "Take care of yourself, and share what you have learned with your hive."

"I will." Dex flew back to the bus and back under Max's collar.

"You were gone a long time, Dex," Max said. "Did you have fun?"

"Not only did I have fun, but I met another bee who just informed me of what my true purpose is in this world."

"Wow," said Max. "We have a bus ride back, so you can tell me on the way."

As the bus made its way back to the school, Dex told Max about his newfound friend, Trint, and all that he had shared with him. "I'm glad I came with you, Max," Dex said. "Thanks for bringing me along."

"No problem. You'll be able to visit this farm again when I visit my grandparents this summer."

"Cool," said Dex. "I can't wait."

Max ate some of the honey, played with some of the souvenirs, and then he dozed off on the school bus.

# CHAPTER TEN

## AN UNEXPECTED TURN OF EVENTS

NATURE'S SUMMER SONG: May had turned into June. Spring had relinquished its hold and handed the reins over to summer. Summer was finally here. The tree leaves were young and green. The new summer morning brought a gentleness that seemed to cover the entire neighborhood like a warm blanket. The sun came up early, so the people could enjoy the summer days longer. Marigolds and lavender flowers sprouted up, and the fragrances spread around the neighborhood. A robin brought food to her newly hatched chicks; their high-pitched chirping added to the sounds of the early summer. Caterpillars emerged from their cocoons to show the world their beautiful transformation into colorful butterflies. They climbed onto the edge of branches to prepare for their maiden flights. Summer . . . had officially arrived.

***

Max and Joanna were out of school for summer vacation. Their excitement clearly showed as soon as they came home. They had collective aspirations of staying up late watching TV and sleeping in late the next morning—the rewards of having gotten good grades and having had good behavior throughout the school year.

Mr. Thomas had summer plans for the family for the first month of summer: amusement parks, picnics at the beach, visits and overnight stays at their grandparents' house, and random trips for ice cream on very hot days. Dex got a chance to experience all the family festivities while hanging out with Max.

The bond between Max and Dex was as strong as ever. The fact that they had to keep it a secret made it more exciting for Max.

Dex still missed being at his hive with the other bees, but being with Max helped him get through those tough days. In fact, Dex felt more confident than ever that living with Max was where he belonged.

Dex was also thinking about the farm. He would love it if his hive could move there someday. Occasionally, he would fly over to his old route to look for Tank. He would watch discreetly as Tank and his new partner would forage. Dex could tell Tank was bored with the other bee, and he knew he was right. Tank clearly missed foraging with his best friend; Dex could see it in Tank's demeanor. Dex missed coming back late and hearing from the queen. That was nothing but a memory now. Dex was on his own, and he now had to fend for himself: a tall task for a bee that was raised to work together with hundreds of other bees.

Sometimes, Max and Dex would sit outside on the

backyard patio at night with the family. Dex had never been outside this late at night when he lived at the hive. Only the guard bees would be outside that late, and that was only near the hive to keep watch.

Dex was fascinated to see insects that he never knew about. He saw crickets chirping in the grass, moths fluttering around the lights by the house, and even a few beetles that he had never seen before that only came out at night.

Dex liked when the family sat outside together; he would hide under Max's collar and listen to them talk. The togetherness and closeness of the family reminded him of his hive.

Sometimes, Max would go out in the back yard by himself and sit and take Dex with him so they could talk and hang out. Max had to be careful not to talk too loudly because Joanna would sneak over and try to catch him talking to himself. She had her suspicions about who he was talking to, but a bee was not one of them. She was determined to find out, and that kept Max on his toes. Dex had to keep watch as well; after all, she had nearly killed him with bug spray.

One day, Max was sitting in the back yard with Dex. It was dusk outside, so there was still a little bit of daylight left. Dex saw flashes of tiny green lights nearby. He then looked around and saw that the tiny lights were also around the entire neighborhood. The tiny green lights flashed on and off and floated around slowly when they flashed on.

"What are those green lights?" he asked.

"Fireflies," Max replied. "Some people call them lightning bugs."

"Fireflies? Are they made of fire?"

Max chuckled. "No, they have a green "glowy" thing on their behinds. When I was younger, I used to catch them and put them in a jar, and it would look like I had a green lantern. Then I would set them free and watch them all fly out."

Dex did not like that Max used to catch the fireflies against their will. "Why would you trap them like that?"

"It was something I used to do when I was younger." Max replied with a shrug.

Just then, Joanna burst outside with a jar. "Ooooh!! Lightning bugs!!! I'm going to catch ALL of them!" Joanna ran down the stairs and took off running past Max and into the back yard with her jar open to catch the lightning bugs.

When Joanna was out of sight, Dex came out and looked at Max with a smirk on his face.

"Well, she is only eight years old," Max said with a shrug. "I'm thirteen now. I've outgrown catching fireflies."

Just then, a firefly flew close to Max. "Watch this," said Max. He stretched out his hand and the firefly landed on it. The firefly walked along Max's fingers and between them. The firefly then moved up his hand and crawled along his arm, then slowly flew away. "See? No harm at all, Dex. The fireflies like us, and we like them."

Dex was amazed that the firefly would even get that close to a human.

While they were looking at the fireflies, a mosquito landed on the back of Max's neck not far from where Dex was sitting. The mosquito was about to prick his neck to drink Max's blood, but then he spotted Dex sitting on his shoulder. The mosquito had never seen this type of insect before. His curiosity outweighed his hunger, and he flew over to talk to Dex.

"What are you?" the mosquito asked.

Dex turned around and saw the mosquito looking at him with a scowl on his face. "I'm a bee," Dex replied.

"Oh, I know about you honey makers," said the mosquito. "I've just never seen one before."

"What are you?"

"I am a mosquito," the mosquito responded proudly. "You're a daytime insect, right?"

"Yes, I am."

"What are you doing out here at night, then?"

Dex didn't want to tell the mosquito he was hanging out with a human, even though he was standing on Max's shoulder, so he lied. "I'm resting," he replied. "Did you come over here to talk to me?"

"No, I came here to feed." The mosquito then flew back to Max's neck and looked over at Dex, placing one of his legs to his mouth. "Shhhh," he whispered. The mosquito then stuck Max with a sharp tube that came out of his face, and he began to drink Max's blood.

"What are you doing?" Dex cried.

"I'm drinking. Now shut up before this human finds out."

Dex was confused. He looked at Max, but Max was still

looking at the fireflies and was unaware that the mosquito was feeding on him.

"Why are you drinking from him?" asked Dex.

The mosquito, clearly annoyed, raised his head up to talk. "I'm drinking from him because I'm hungry, but you won't shut your m—"

SMACK!!!!

Max's hand came across and hit the mosquito with such a force that it killed him instantly.

Dex watched in shock as the mosquito's lifeless body fell to the ground. "Why did you kill him, Max?" Dex cried.

"It was a mosquito," Max replied. "It bit me."

"I was talking to him, and you killed him like he was nothing!" Dex yelled. He then remembered how Max had picked up his shoe when he had first spoken with him. "Oh my goodness! You would've done that to me with that shoe!"

"Dex, please calm down and let me explain," Max pleaded.

"Or what? You're gonna smack me like you did that poor mosquito?"

"The mosquito bit me; it was drinking my blood! Come on. Let's go inside and I can explain."

Dex shook his head, jumped off Max's shoulder and flew a short distance from him. "I—I don't think I can go back in with you, Max."

"What are you talking about? You want to leave? Where will you go? You can't go back to your hive, and it's too dangerous out here at night, especially for a bee who's not used to being out here. Don't do this, Dex. I'm begging you. I don't want something bad to happen to you out here."

Dex looked at Max and shook his head. "I'm sorry, Max. Maybe this was not a good idea for me to live with you. Yes, it is dangerous out here, but it's just as dangerous in your house as well. Your sister tried to kill me, you just killed that mosquito right in front of me as if it was nothing, and you were going to kill me with that shoe when we first met. I would rather take my chances outside on my own. I don't know where I will go. All I know is I just need to be alone right now, Max. Goodbye." Dex turned and flew away.

Max looked around and realized he was outside by himself. Joanna had already gone back in the house. Max sat outside for a while longer to see if Dex would come back, but he finally realized he was not coming back. Max went back inside, ran to his room, and cried himself to sleep.

# CHAPTER ELEVEN

## A DAY AT THE PARK

Dex was flying around very cautiously. Except for the streetlights, it was too dark for him to see, and he was clearly afraid. Maybe he shouldn't have left—at least not this late at night.

He could still see Max's hand hitting that mosquito, replaying over and over in his mind. What had that mosquito done to deserve such a harsh death? Dex knew he had to stop thinking about it for now because he had to find somewhere to sleep tonight. He was really thinking about his bed that Max had made for him; it had been so soft and cozy. *Maybe I should've stayed, at least through the night,* he thought.

It was too late for him to go back to Max's house. Right now, he needed to find somewhere to sleep—and fast. Being outside at night was no place for a single bee. The dangers were elevated at night, and there were many more predators out here.

After what seemed like hours of searching, Dex found his way to a park. It was too dark to see anything because all the lights were turned off for the evening, but he managed to spot an unused plastic cup lying on a picnic table. Dex checked around to make sure the area was safe. He crawled inside the cup. He was finally about to get some rest.

It wasn't long before Dex was awakened by a low rumbling sound in the distance. He crawled out of the cup and saw flashes of lightning racing across the sky. A storm was coming, and Dex did not have a sturdy shelter. He quickly left the plastic cup and flew around until he found refuge on the underside of one of the plastic play gyms. He bunkered in just as the rain started to fall.

***

Max awoke to the sound of a thunderstorm. He quickly jumped out of bed and opened the window. He was worried about Dex being outside. The storm was in full force, and Max was hoping that it would draw Dex back to his house. The only thing Max could do was to wait the storm out and hope Dex survived it.

***

Morning arrived, and Dex woke up to find the entire park soaking wet. There was also litter everywhere: burger wrappers, plastic cups, wet napkins, uneaten food, and clothing left behind. Everything was a wet mess at the park, thanks to the storm.

Dex left the park to find some nectar. He flew over to a nearby garden for a quick fill-up. After he was done, he looked around and realized that he really had nothing to do for the rest of the day. Suddenly, Dex felt bored, and it was still only morning. He didn't want to go back to Max's house. He was still upset with Max for killing the mosquito.

Dex still pondered how humans could kill insects so easily and thoughtlessly. He had thought Max was different, that Max was a human who could be trusted to be nice to insects. Maybe the queen was right: humans really could not be trusted. He didn't know if he would ever talk to or visit Max again.

Dex decided to pass the time by exploring other neighborhoods. After all, he had no curfew or obligations to uphold, so he could come and go as he pleased.

As the morning drew on, it became hotter. Children were starting to come out, and soon the neighborhoods were alive with children and adults enjoying the hot weather once again. Dex watched from the top of a light pole and chuckled to himself remembering how Tank would always sit on top of the light pole to watch the humans. Now, he found himself doing the same thing.

Dex was still thinking about Tank, when suddenly, he was interrupted by the scream of a little girl.

"It stung me! It stung me!" she cried. She was holding her arm and running toward her mother who was in her front yard. The mother picked up the little girl, and they both went into the house.

Dex saw two wasps flying away. One of them had stung her.

"See, I told you she was going to cry," the wasp sneered to the other one. They both flew away, laughing and joking about the little girl that had been stung.

Dex was furious. "That was a mean thing that wasp did to that poor little girl," he said to himself. He decided to return to the park where he had slept. All the trash was cleaned up, and the park was dry. People were starting to show up and set up their picnics.

Dex spent most of the afternoon watching the people. Everybody was having a good time: Kids were running around, some people were tossing footballs and Frisbees, and some sat on their fold-out chairs to bask in the warm sun.

Dex watched as some ants crawled out of a hole in the ground. He flew to a lower branch to get a better look at them. The ants marched in a military-like formation. They were synchronized and disciplined, prepared for what seemed like a battle.

The leader ant spotted Dex on the lower branch, commanded the ants to stop, and spoke to Dex. "Stand to, soldier, and state your name!"

"Hi, I'm Dex."

"I'm the leader of this platoon. They call me The General Ant, but you can just call me General."

"Nice to meet you, General," said Dex.

"I hate to cut this greeting short, but we need food," General said. "Those civilians have ALL the food we want!" He then quickly hurried to the front of his platoon and yelled: "ATTENTION!!! FORWARRRDDDD . . . MARCH!!!"

The ants began to march, heading toward an open picnic basket that a family had left on the ground not far away. They had forgotten to close the basket, and had put it on the table before taking a walk.

"It's time to take what is rightfully ours!" General

shouted.

"But that's not your food," Dex argued.

"Stand down, honeybee!" General shouted. "Insubordination will *NOT* be tolerated!" He turned to his platoon. "Get as much food as you can! Attack anything that tries to compromise our mission!"

The ants heeded and then commenced to raid the picnic basket. Shortly after the ants began their raid, Dex saw a group of flies headed for the basket.

"Look, an unattended picnic basket . . . and it's open . . . with no humans in sight!" cried one of the flies. "This is our lucky day!"

Dex watched in disbelief as dozens of flies landed on an uncovered sandwich in the basket. The dirty, dusty flies walked all over the sandwich with their hairy feet. They puked all over the food to dissolve it, and then they slurped the liquefied food with their long, sticky tongues.

The ants and the flies soon began to conflict with each other on all the food. Some of the ants broke ranks to fend off the flies, as the rest of them carried off chunks of food to their nest. The ants and flies were ruining the food the family had left behind. By the time the family came back, all the food in the picnic basket was covered with hundreds of ants and dozens of flies. The food in the basket was no longer edible.

The father quickly picked up the basket to throw it away, and the flies flew off in a hurry. Many of the ants began to bite the father as he approached the trashcan.

"Bite to the death!" shouted General. "This food is ours!" The father tossed the basket into the trashcan and shook off the remaining ants that were biting his hand.

The flies spotted the food in the trashcan and immediately dove in to eat. The ants and flies continued their battle in the trashcan over the newly tossed food and all the scraps that were already in there.

Dex could not believe what he had just witnessed. That poor family had to leave the picnic because the ants and the flies had ruined all their food. He was beginning to see how his fellow insects were being a nuisance to humans. He wondered why he had never seen this in the beginning or even while he was hanging out with Max and his family.

Dex flew over to another area of the park to observe how insects and humans interacted with each other. He started to notice the humans swatting at bugs constantly when they tried to land on them or their food. He also noticed the flies and gnats were the most persistent offenders to the humans when it came to annoying them.

The flies flew into the faces of the humans for no reason at all. The humans would swat at the tiny, annoying gnats to drive them away, but that did not work. The gnats just kept coming at them, trying to land on their food. Some of the flies were too slow in getting away as the humans swatted them but it didn't stop the other flies from attacking.

Dex actually didn't feel too bad when the flies were getting swatted after witnessing how annoying they were.

***

Later that evening, as the sun was going down, most of the flies had retreated to their hideouts, and the ants were back in their homes. Dex welcomed the cool, gentle breeze, as did the humans at the park.

He was watching a little boy run back and forth from tree to tree. The boy then ran to the tree where Dex was resting. Suddenly, the boy stopped and he smacked the back of his neck...exactly the way Max had when that mosquito had landed on him. The boy looked at his hand, and lying in his palm was a dead mosquito that had bitten him.

Dex suddenly heard little buzzing sounds in the air. He looked up and saw hundreds upon hundreds of mosquitoes forming clusters and branching out toward the humans to feed on them.

One of the mosquitoes landed on the branch Dex was sitting on and spoke to him. "I don't usually see bees out here this late," he said.

"You know what I am?" asked Dex.

"Of course I do," said the mosquito. "You're a bumble bee."

"Honeybee," Dex corrected.

"Whatever," snapped the mosquito. "Bumblebee, honeybee—it don't matter. All you do is buzz around raiding flowers! I'm older, so I can call you whatever I want!"

Dex shook his head and shrugged. "Why do you feed on the humans?"

"The same reason why you make honey. It's in our nature."

"But the humans can kill you while you feed on them," Dex argued.

"The humans can kill you too, just by being in their way," the mosquito retorted. "We feed on the blood of humans and animals. It's just who we are. We bite 'em, and they break out with an itchy bump. So, of course they don't like to get bitten by us."

The old mosquito continued watching the boy, who was

slowly going to sleep. The child, who was lying in his mother's arms, was fighting sleep and kept waking up.

"Why are you sitting up here with me?" asked Dex. "Shouldn't you be out there feeding with the rest of the mosquitoes?"

The old mosquito laughed. "Ah, young bee. While those young'uns are out there chasing their meals, I'm waiting on mine to stay still. It is called patience, my young friend."

The mosquito saw that the boy had finally gone to sleep. "Gotta go young'un," said the mosquito. "My meal is finally asleep."

The old mosquito flashed a sly grin, flew off the branch, and landed on the sleeping boy. He crawled along the boy's arm, looking for an ideal spot to feed. When he found his choice spot, he pierced the boy's arm with his trunk and began to drink. Other mosquitoes joined in, feeding on the little boy's flesh for several seconds, but then the child's mother saw them and brushed them off.

Dex had seen enough for one day. He had seen all he needed to see from the human's point of view and now had a new understanding of why humans had a dislike for some insects. The humans were protecting themselves, and they were guarding their food from them.

Dex was no longer upset at Max; he now understood him and needed to go back to let him know.

Dex flew quickly back to Max's house, arriving to find the window closed and the lights out. He peered through the window, but he could not see inside, so he waited a few minutes. After some time, Max came into his room, turned on the light, jumped into the bed, and turned on the TV. He didn't even open the window.

Dex waited some more. Finally, Max looked over and noticed the window was closed, so he went over and opened

it, then walked back to his bed and flopped back down.

Dex flew in and landed on the desk. "Hi, Max."

Max quickly jumped up and closed his door. "You're back!" Max said excitedly. "I was so worried about you. I'm sorry about what I did last night."

"No, It's me that owes you the apology. I didn't understand you and what humans go through when it comes to insects. For that, I am sorry, Max. Hey, let me see your neck." Dex quickly flew behind the boy and looked at his neck. He could see a small, reddish bump where the mosquito had bitten him the night before. "Does that bump itch?"

"Of course it does," Max replied. Then he squinted at Dex. "Something happened out there, didn't it?"

"Let's just say I will never annoy you like other insects do." Dex spent a good part of the night telling Max about the flies, the ants, the gnats, and the mosquitoes that had wreaked havoc on the humans at the park earlier that day.

# CHAPTER TWELVE

## TROUBLING NEWS

The queen was up earlier than normal at her throne, deep in thought, trying to come up with ways to improve the quality of life in the hive. She thought about new safety measures. She thought about the expansion of the hive, as space was getting tight. She thought that perhaps the next summer they could possibly move to a bigger hive.

She also thought about Dex. A lot of time had passed, and she hadn't heard anything from Tank about him because Tank had not seen Dex since she had banished him from the hive. She worried about him, but she felt she had done the right thing. Dex had compromised the security of the hive, and she believed that the punishment was just.

A guard bee suddenly flew in with urgent news. "Your Majesty, humans have been spotted in the field near the hive."

"How close?" the queen asked.

"Several meters away," the guard bee replied. "Not close enough to launch an attack. They appear to be looking for something."

"Are they wearing yellow hats?" asked the queen.

"Yes," replied the guard bee.

“Send out the scouts to begin the search for a new home, now!” commanded the queen. “Keep a close watch on those humans, and I want a report on the hour.”

“Yes, Your Majesty.”

***

That very moment, Max was eating breakfast with his family, and Dex was in his usual place under Max’s collar.

Mr. Thomas was reading the local news on his tablet, when he came across an article that made him squint with curiosity. “Cora, you know that big empty lot on the other side of the neighborhood . . . the place with all that tall, dry grass?” he asked.

“Yeah, I remember that place,” Mrs. Thomas replied.

“I just read that they are finally going to clear that lot out, trees and all. They are going to build an apartment complex.”

Dex heard Mr. Thomas talk about the empty lot, which sounded a lot like his home. He began to feel nervous and scared and started to buzz and shake with worry. Max felt the vibrations on his neck, so he quickly excused himself from the table and hurried outside.

"What's the matter, Dex?" asked Max.

"That article your father just read is talking about my home!" Dex exclaimed. "They are going to destroy my home!"

"Oh no! You have to warn your hive before it's too late."

"I'm exiled, so I can't go back to the hive. I have to find Tank. I'll tell him, and he can warn the queen. I'll be back." He quickly flew to his old route to find Tank.

Max walked back into the house to get more information on the future construction at the empty lot.

***

Dex found Tank and his new partner at one of their rest stops.

"Tank, you have to listen to me! This is important!" he cried, out of breath.

"Dex!" Tank exclaimed excitedly. "How have you been? This is my new partner, Brandon. You remember him, don't you? Why do you look like you've just seen a ghost?"

Dex caught his breath. "Hi, Brandon. How's it going? It's good to see you. Tank, our home is in danger."

"Whoa, Dex! Slow down!" said Tank. "Did you just say our home is in danger?"

"Yes. The humans are going to start building an apartment complex where we live."

"Did your human friend put you up to this trick, Dex?" asked Brandon.

"Why would I joke about something as serious as this?" snapped Dex. "Just warn the queen that you have to move out before it's too late."

Tank looked at Brandon. "Maybe it's worth it to tell the queen," he suggested.

"We can tell her after we're done foraging," said Brandon.

"No, we need to tell the queen now," Tank argued. "This is too important to ignore."

Brandon nodded in agreement. "Ok, ok."

"I hope you are wrong about this, Dex," Tank told Dex before flying away.

"I hope I am too," Dex said. "I'll meet up with you tomorrow."

Tank and Brandon headed back to the hive, and Dex flew back to Max's house.

***

Max was waiting for Dex when he came back. "Dex, we have to save your hive, fast. The construction workers are going to start clearing out the field sometime next week."

Dex didn't know what to do. He did not want to see his home destroyed. Even though he was exiled from the hive, those bees were still his family.

***

Tank and Brandon arrived at the queen's throne out of breath.

"Your Majesty, we have some urgent news to bring to your attention," Tank panted.

"You may speak."

"I saw Dex today—"

The queen quickly stood up from her throne. "How is he?" she inquired.

"He is fine, Your Majesty," Tank replied. "But he told me the hive was in danger, and that we had to move."

The queen looked away for a second, shook her head, and then looked back at Tank. "I know, Tank. I have already sent out scouts to look for a new home."

Tank was confused. "My Queen, how did you know?"

"I am all too familiar with this situation," replied the queen.

Tank and Brandon looked at each other and squinted in confusion. "I don't understand, Your Majesty," said Tank.

"Our last home was destroyed by humans dressed like the ones that were seen this morning," the queen explained. "You were a larva and too young to remember, Tank. Our old hive was in a tree in a bigger field, much like where we live now. Some humans, wearing yellow hats, came looking around; and a couple weeks later, they arrived with large machines. They were digging, ripping, and tearing everything apart. Lots of animals and insects could not escape the terror that happened that day. The remaining animals and insects had to evacuate. Tank, I carried you and Dex as we searched for a new home. I worked in the nursery before I was anointed as a queen."

Tank's jaw dropped. "You never mentioned that you cared for Dex and me."

The queen smiled. "You and Dex were my assigned larvae," she said glowingly. "I fed you, nurtured you, and cared for you. Shortly after we moved here, I was anointed to be queen, and I had to be groomed so I could eventually take over the hive. I had to leave the nursery. I watched you two grow up from a distance. It really hurt me to exile Dex, but I did what I had to do for the welfare of the hive. Sometimes a queen has to make tough decisions, and that was one of the toughest I had to make, regarding Dex."

"I understand, my Queen," said Tank. "Right now, we have to find another home before it's too late. I'm going to meet up with Dex tomorrow to see if we can come up with a solution." Then he and Brandon quickly left the queen's throne.

***

Dex and Max were in Max's room conversing about how to save the hive.

"The queen has probably sent the scouts out to search for a new home," said Dex.

"Is there anywhere else you can think of that the scouts might not know about?"

Dex thought long and hard, and then suddenly he had it. "The farm!" he exclaimed. "We can live at the farm!"

Joanna suddenly burst into Max's room. "A-HA!" she yelled. "I finally caught you! You're talking to a bug! Eww, gross! I'm telling Daddy!"

Max jumped up, grabbed Joanna by the arm, and closed the door, while Dex quickly flew out the window, as he was afraid Joanna would try to hurt him again.

"Listen, Joanna," Max whispered frantically. "You have to keep quiet on this one. The bee I'm talking to is really friendly; he's not going to hurt you."

"Why are you talking to a bee?" asked Joanna. "That's just silly."

"I know it sounds silly, but it's true. He was trapped in a spider's web, and I rescued him; then he followed me home and spoke to me. We've been friends ever since."

"You mean that bee can talk?" Joanna narrowed her eyes, unbelieving.

"Yes." Max looked out the window. "Dex, where are you?" he called. He then looked back at Joanna. "You have to promise me you won't tell Mom or Dad."

"Okay," Joanna agreed. "I guess this will also be the last day you pull my ponytails . . .*forever* . . . if you don't want me to tell on you."

"It's a deal," said Max. "Dex, it's safe to come in now." Dex slowly flew in and landed on Max's desk.

Joanna folded her arms. "I wanna hear him talk," she demanded.

"Dex, say something," Max ordered. Dex did not speak. "Dex, come on, please?" Max begged.

Dex slowly walked in a circle, fanned his wings, and then he buzzed. Max slapped the palm of his hand to his forehead in frustration.

"Is the wittle bee afwaid to talk?" Joanna sneered using a baby voice. She walked to the door and opened it. "Oooohhhh, D-a-a-a-a-dddy," she said quietly.

Max grabbed Joanna's arm again and pulled her back in.

"Look, he's nervous," he pleaded. "His home is in danger, and we have to act fast."

"Not my concern," Joanna snuffed. "The deal is off. I'm telling Daddy."

"Please—I need his help," Dex finally spoke. "My home is in serious danger. We're wasting time right now. I have to find a home for my family. Will you help me?"

Joanna stood frozen with her mouth open wide. "Oh my goodness! You really CAN talk!" Joanna closed Max's door and slowly walked over to Dex. He cautiously walked backward.

"Are you the same bee I sprayed a while back?" she asked.

"Yes."

Joanna looked at Max, and then she looked back at Dex. "I'm sorry I sprayed you."

"That's okay. I understand you hate insects."

"I will help you find a new home," said Joanna.

"Thank you so much, Joanna," Dex sighed with relief.

"Okay, so there's room at the farm, right?" asked Max.

"Yes. Trint already said there was plenty of room for our hive," Dex confirmed.

"I can ask Daddy to take us to the farm," Joanna suggested.

"Good idea, Sis," said Max. "I'll talk to the beekeeper about rescuing Dex's hive."

"What about me?" asked Dex.

"You are going to have to go back to your hive and convince the queen to let the beekeeper take the bees to the farm," Max replied.

Dex sighed. He knew he had the toughest part of the plan, but Dex was willing to do whatever it took to save his hive—even if it meant risking a possible attack from the very bees he was trying to help save.

# CHAPTER THIRTEEN

## THE PLAN

Joanna ran downstairs to look for her dad. "Daddy!" she yelled. "Where are you?"

"I'm in the living room, Joanna."

Joanna ran in the room and hopped onto her father's lap. "Can you take me to the farm?" she asked.

"Didn't you just go to the farm not too long ago?" Mr. Thomas inquired.

"No, that was Max."

"Well, I guess we can go then."

"Good! So we're going tomorrow! Thanks, Daddy!" said Joanna excitedly.

"Tomorrow?" Mr. Thomas repeated.

Joanna kissed her dad on the cheek and quickly ran upstairs. "Hey, Max! We're going to the farm tomorrow! *Yipeeeee!!!!*"

Mr. Thomas shook his head and chuckled. "I guess we are going tomorrow, and Max is coming with us."

Joanna went to Max's room and closed the door. "Daddy is taking us tomorrow."

"Good," said Max. "It's on you now, Dex."

Dex gulped. Tomorrow was going to be a big day for him.

The future of the hive now depended on whether he could convince the queen to trust the humans to help them.

***

Later that night, Dex lay in his ring box bed wide awake. He was deep in thought wondering how the queen would react about trusting a human to help them move. He would first have to gain access to the hive because he was banned and feared the guards would attack him on sight. He thought if Tank and Brandon escorted him, the guards would hold off on their potential attack.

The morning came and Dex awoke, took a deep breath, and climbed out of his bed.

Max was already awake. "Nervous?"

"Very," Dex admitted.

"Everything will work out for the best."

"I hope so," said Dex. "I better get going. Tank and Brandon are probably foraging now, and I have to meet them."

Dex soon met up with Tank and Brandon at one of their rest stops on a windowsill. "I need to talk to the queen," said Dex.

"How are you going to do that, Dex? You're banned," Brandon reminded him.

"You two are going to escort me to the hive," Dex explained. "The future of our hive depends on the information I have for the queen. I found a potential home, and it's going to be up to her if she wants us to move there."

Tank looked at Brandon and Brandon shrugged. "Okay, Dex; let's do it," Tank agreed. "We'll escort you to the queen, but after that, it's on you. Let's go."

As they flew closer to the hive, Dex grew nervous. Although he had Tank and Brandon escorting him, he still thought he would face some kind of attack from the guard bees. When the guard bees did not attack, he breathed a sigh of relief.

As they approached the hive opening, one of the guard bees spoke to them. "Well, well, well, two forager bees leave to bring back nectar; and instead, they come back with a traitor!"

All three bees ignored the guard bee as they headed for the queen's throne room. When the queen saw Dex, she had to restrain herself from being overly emotional. She had missed him, but she had to keep her composure. "Hello, Dex," she greeted with a no-nonsense voice. "You are banned; therefore, it's a great risk for you to be here. I take it that you have some very important news to bring to my attention that is worth risking an attack from the guard bees."

"Your Majesty," Dex began. "I am aware of my situation. I came here because I have a possible solution that can save the hive." Just as he was about to explain, the scouts came in with a report for the queen.

"Your Majesty—I'm afraid I have bad news to report," the head scout stated. "All the scouts have come back with negative results. There is no place suitable for us to move to."

Dex stepped forward next to the head scout. "I know of a place that this hive can move to."

The head scout looked over at Dex with disdain. "The traitor found a place for us to live? And where might that be . . . in the human's basement?"

"My Queen, you have to trust me," Dex pleaded.

The head scout scoffed. "Are you seriously entertaining this traitor's claim about finding a home? Did you not ban him for bringing a human near our hive?"

Dex could feel his knees shake with nervousness. The last thing he wanted was a reminder of why he was banned in the first place. His solution was going to involve human help.

But then, Dex grew angry with the head scout. It seemed most of the bees spent more time focusing on him being a traitor rather than finding a solution to save the hive. He turned to the head scout bravely. "Shut up!" yelled Dex. "Our hive is about to be demolished, and all you bees keep talking about is me being a traitor!"

Dex turned back to the queen. "There is a farm too far for us to go by flight. I met another bee there a few weeks ago who told me there is plenty of room for our hive to live. They have humans who help take care of them and they are called beekeepers." All the bees in the throne room gasped. Dex continued. "The human I've been living with is on his way to the farm as we speak. They are going to send the beekeeper to come and get us to take us to the farm."

"You sent more humans to come to our home?" the queen challenged angrily.

"Yes," Dex replied boldly. "We need their help. I don't intend to disrespect you, my Queen, but I think you are too proud to admit this hive needs outside help." The queen scowled at Dex but let him continue. "The bee at the farm explained to me how we provide for the humans and how the humans provide for us."

"Do explain," snapped the head scout. *"This, I have got to hear."*

"The humans plant the flowers," Dex explained. "We, the bees, pollinate the flowers, and the flowers are then able to produce more flowers. In most cases, like on the farm, the bees help produce more crops for the animals and the humans."

"You mean to tell me that the humans, the plants, and the bees all work together, like in a cycle?" the queen asked.

"Yes, Your Majesty," Dex replied. "Ultimately, you have the final say. The farm is the place where this hive can flourish. Not all humans are bad to us, and not all insects are good to the humans. I have seen this with my own compound eyes. It's time to put our petty differences aside and start thinking about the future of this hive."

The queen looked at Dex with admiration. She had never seen this side of him before. He was no longer the fun-loving, careless bee who loved to fly fast, looking for dandelion nectar. He was maturing into an outspoken leader who cared deeply for the hive, even though most of the hive was against him. She looked at Tank and saw how much he, too, had grown in his maturity over the past few months.

"My two larvae have grown into leaders," the queen boasted.

"Your two larvae?" Dex turned to Tank with a confused

look on his face.

"I'll explain later," said Tank.

The queen stood up and deeply sighed. "Dex, as tough as a decision this is for me to make, I am going to trust you. We will allow the humans to take us to the farm. Go tell the human we will not attack. We will not put up a resistance."

Dex smiled at the queen. "You will not be disappointed, My Queen."

***

Meanwhile, Mr. Thomas, Max, and Joanna were taking the tour of the farm.

"I can't wait to see the bees!" Joanna exclaimed.

"I thought you hated insects?" Mr. Thomas asked.

"Oh, I like bees now," Joanna replied.

Max nudged Joanna. "Will you be quiet?"

"Sorry, Max," Joanna whispered.

They finally reached the beehive portion of the tour. Max saw the beekeeper walk by and quickly tugged on the man's shirt. "Excuse me, sir. I have a problem."

"What is it young man?"

"There is a hive in an empty lot near my house that is in danger," Max explained. "They are going to start construction sometime this week, and if someone doesn't rescue those bees, they are going to lose their home."

"Can you rescue the little bees, Mr. Beekeeper?" asked Joanna. "You can bring them here, can't you?"

The beekeeper smiled at Joanna. "Yes, we can. I'll see what we can do."

Max gave the beekeeper the address to the empty lot, and the beekeeper went into his office.

"So, you brought me all the way out here to save some bees?" Mr. Thomas asked.

"Yes, Daddy!" Joanna cried excitedly. Mr. Thomas looked at Max for confirmation.

"This is important to us, Dad. We don't want them to lose their home."

Mr. Thomas smiled at his two kids. “I’m proud of you two. Those bees are lucky to have you two in their corner.”

Mr. Thomas hugged his kids, and they headed back home.

# CHAPTER FOURTEEN

## TROUBLE IN THE FIELD

Max rested his head against the window in the car. His plan was working well so far, but he wondered how Dex was holding up on the most difficult part of this plan. He wondered if Dex had even made it into the hive because of the possible attack from his own bees.

Max realized he was thinking too much about it and quickly dismissed his thoughts. He would be home soon and would meet up with Dex.

When the family made it home, Max raced upstairs to his room, and Joanna followed.

"Where is Dex?" Joanna asked.

"He's probably still at his hive," Max replied. "Hopefully, everything turned out fine and he's on his way back."

Minutes later, Dex returned.

"Wow, perfect timing," said Max. "We just got home a little while ago. So how did things go with the queen?"

"She is willing to let the beekeeper take the hive, and she will not order an attack."

"Nice!" Max exclaimed.

"We did it!" Joanna shouted.

"Now, we have to wait for the beekeeper to get here

before the construction workers show up," Max said.

"I'm guessing everything went well at the farm," said Dex.

"I gave the beekeeper the address, and I told him to get here before the construction starts," Max said. "It's up to him to get here."

***

Back at the hive, the queen was having second thoughts about letting the humans come to take them to the farm. She wondered how the humans would treat the bees at the farm. After all, she was making a decision that would affect the entire hive.

The queen heard humans talking outside the hive. Curious, she flew to the hive opening and out into the open. It was common for the queen to go outside to get some fresh air from time to time. It was, however, uncommon for the queen to go outside alone—especially when there were humans nearby.

One of the guard bees flew over to escort her, but the queen shook her head. "No need for an escort today."

"Your Majesty, there are humans out here," the guard bee argued.

The queen smiled. "I am perfectly capable of taking care of myself. I have not forgotten how to use my stinger, young bee." The queen continued past the guard bee. She wanted to know more about the humans' plans. Perhaps she could listen in on them to find out exactly when they were coming with their big machines.

Spotting a group of workers standing by a small tree, the queen quietly flew in close and landed on one of the lower branches just above their heads and listened in.

"This place is an absolute dump," said one of the workers.

"Yes, it is," another worker agreed.

"I'm glad we're starting early so we can get this job done early," chimed in another person.

The boss walked over and spoke to the group. "All right, folks. All the plans are drawn out. We have the landscapers coming by tomorrow to mow this tall grass down. Then, on Monday, we can start taking these trees down."

The queen had heard enough. She had all the intel she needed. She was about to fly away when she was spotted by one of the workers.

"It's a bee!" he cried. He quickly took off his hard hat and began to swing wildly at the queen, but he missed repeatedly. "I hate bees!" he yelled as he began chasing the queen.

She flew up high to keep her distance from the worker. "This guy is not giving up," she said to herself. The queen finally made it to the hive, and the worker stopped immediately in his tracks.

"Whoa. This chase ends here," he said quietly. The worker did not want to disturb the hive, so he slowly retreated to the group.

The queen, out of breath, laughed to herself.

"What is so funny, Your Majesty?" the guard bee asked.

"I haven't had an adventure like that in quite some time," she replied. "Send for Tank. There is much to discuss."

Tank soon arrived at the throne, and the queen explained: "I overheard the humans talking today. They plan on mowing the grass tomorrow and will begin cutting the trees on Monday."

"That's only a few days!" Tank cried. "I'll tell Dex. I'm meeting up with him later."

***

When Tank and Dex met up, Tank told him the news, and Dex relayed it to Max.

"I have an idea," said Max. "Maybe the queen can let me take the hive until the beekeeper comes."

"Are you nuts, Max? The queen will never allow that to happen!"

"Well, we don't know when the beekeeper is coming, and it might be too late when he does!" Max exclaimed. "We have to do something. At least ask her, Dex."

"I'm not asking her. She will say no. She will not allow it."

"We have a tree in our back yard," Max continued. "The hive can hang out there. I can tell the beekeeper to come to our house and pick them up."

"No," Dex replied adamantly. "I already told you: the queen will not allow it. I'm sorry."

Max was upset that Dex would not even try to ask the queen to let him bring the hive to his back yard, so he decided to take matters into his own hands. He was going to approach the hive by himself, even if it meant risking a possible attack from hundreds of angry bees. It was a risk Max was willing to take to save Dex's hive.

***

Early the next morning, Max woke up and immediately looked over at Dex's bed. The bee was still asleep. Max snuck out the room, tiptoed downstairs, and left the house. He hopped on his bike and rode towards the hive.

On the way there, Max wondered what he would say. He knew the bees would recognize him, and he knew they would understand him, even though they would not talk back to him. Max figured he would just wing it; whatever came to his mind is what he would say.

Max arrived at the field and pulled out his dad's binoculars. Peering through the lenses, he saw the hive. He also could see that he could climb the tree to get to the hive if he needed to because it wasn't that far off the ground. Taking a deep breath, he left his bike and began to walk slowly through the tall dry grass. "Please don't sting me, please don't sting me, please don't sting me," Max said quietly to himself. He knew by now that the guard bees would have spotted him, so he put both hands in the air to show he was not a threat to them. Still, this was no guarantee he would not be attacked by the bees.

Max waded slowly through the grass, feeling it brush against his legs. It was very itchy and rough.

By now, the guard bees had informed the queen about an intruder approaching the hive. The queen realized it was the human that Dex lived with.

"Our soldiers are in position to attack on your command, Your Majesty," the lead soldier bee informed.

The queen was about to give her command to attack, when she looked at Max again. She noticed that he had his hands up. He didn't appear to be approaching in a threatening manner. "Tell the soldiers to stand down," ordered the queen. "He's not a threat."

"Dex is not with the boy, Your Majesty," said Tank as he came in. "I think he is trying to communicate with us."

The queen ordered all the bees into the hive to be safe. "If the human speaks, I will hear him out," she announced.

Max finally made it to the hive, his knees shaking with nervousness. He could hear the hive buzzing and humming. He took a deep breath, and he spoke: "I'm here to talk to you. My name is Max. Dex has been living with me. I mean you no harm; I only want to help you and save your hive. I have a tree in my back yard and can move you there until the beekeeper comes."

There was no answer from the hive.

"I don't expect you to talk back to me," Max continued. "I know you can hear and understand me. Please let me help you. If you thought I was a threat, I would have been attacked by now."

Max waited a few more minutes. He realized the queen would not cooperate with him, so he turned to walk away. He took a few steps, but suddenly lost his balance and fell into the deep, tall grass.

Max had stepped into a small hole in the ground, and his right foot was trapped inside. Max tried for several minutes to free himself, but his foot was completely lodged.

"This sucks," Max said to himself. "What a bad start to my morning."

Suddenly, Max heard several truck doors close on the other side of the field and could hear some people talking in the distance. He could barely make out what they were saying. Max began to yell to get their attention, but no one heard him; he was too far on the other side of the field. Shortly after he stopped yelling, he heard motors starting up.

Max sat up and realized that those motors were lawnmowers. The landscapers, with large mowers and very loud, had arrived, and they were here to cut the grass. Max's calls for help were being drowned out by the sounds.

He turned his attention to his trapped leg, trying frantically to free himself, but to no avail. Max was afraid. He was at the field all by himself, his foot completely stuck in the ground, he was surrounded by tall grass, and no one knew where he was.

To make matters worse, large lawnmowers were heading in his direction, and the men driving them could not see him.

The queen, Tank, and the rest of the bees watched in horror as the lawnmowers slowly drew closer to Max. Although the bees didn't care too much for humans, they did not want to see a human get hurt . . . or worse.

"We have to do something!" the queen cried.

Tank thought for a minute, and then he came up with

an

idea. "I've got it!" he exclaimed. "If we all come out and form a swarm, that might make the drivers stop. Once he turns off the lawnmower, then the driver will hear the boy."

The queen quickly ordered all the bees out of the hive, and they formed outside.

Max could hear the lawnmowers getting closer. He continued to yell, but they didn't stop. He suddenly looked up and saw the bees coming out of the hive, forming into a swarm.

"Oh, great," he said to himself. "Not only will I be getting run over by a lawnmower, but I'll be getting stung as well."

One of the lawnmowers turned and now was on a direct path towards Max. Max continued to try to free himself.

"Should we go now?" asked the queen.

"Not yet," Tank replied. "It's not close enough yet."

"If it gets too close, it might be too late to stop it!" yelled the queen.

"It has to be stopped close enough for the driver to see or hear Max," Tank insisted.

When the lawnmower was a few yards away from Max, Tank commanded the bees to swarm. "Now!" he screamed.

All the bees flew toward the lawnmower. The landscaper saw the swarming bees flying in his direction, quickly stopped the lawnmower and turned off the engine, then began to run in the opposite direction.

Max was still crying out for help, but now the driver

could hear him. He stopped and turned around, then noticed that the bees had retreated to the hive. He could not see Max, but he followed the boy's voice and soon found him stuck in the ground. He quickly motioned to the other drivers to stop, and they came over to free Max from the hole in the ground.

"Thank you for saving me," Max said.

"Kid, what were you doing out here?" asked one of the landscapers.

"I was trying to save that beehive," Max replied. He then pointed up to the hive in the tree.

"Kid, I hate to break it to you, but those bees actually saved YOUR life," said the first landscaper. "If I had not disturbed those bees, I would have never stopped my lawnmower, and you could have been seriously injured—or worse. I'm still wondering why those bees didn't sting me."

"Well, we can't finish this job when there is a live beehive here," the other landscaper mentioned. "We have to call a beekeeper."

"I already called one," Max said. "They will be here sometime this week."

"Well, that settles it. They cannot build unless we cut this grass, and we are not cutting this grass until somebody moves this hive away. Let's go home, boys!"

The landscapers loaded the lawnmowers into their trucks and left. Max looked up at the hive and smiled. "I know you won't talk back to me, but I want to thank you for saving my life." He walked to his bike just as Dex showed up.

"Max, what are you doing here?" Dex asked.

"Trying to save the hive. But the hive saved me instead." "I'll talk to Tank about it, but right now, you need to go home," Dex said. "Your parents are looking for you."

"Oh, no!" Max exclaimed. "I have to hurry up and get back!" He quickly hopped on his bike and pedaled off to his house.

Dex flew to the hive and met up with Tank. "What's going on over here?"

"Boy did you miss it!" said Tank with excitement. "Your human friend came here to rescue us, but he got his foot stuck in a hole in the ground. Then we swarmed the lawnmower driver so he wouldn't run him over. In a nutshell, that boy just spared us a few more days."

"Wow, I missed all of that?" asked Dex.

"Yeah, where were you?" Tank asked. "I slept in this morning," Dex replied.

"Well, that must be nice," Tank said.

***

Max made it back home to find both of his parents waiting for him.

"Where have you been, Max?" Mrs. Thomas asked, with a scowl on her face.

Max gulped. "I went to the field to check on the bees." "You went without me!" Joanna yelled from upstairs.

"Quiet, Joanna!" ordered Mr. Thomas.

"Why did you go out without telling us?" Mrs. Thomas asked.

"It was too early, and both of you were asleep," Max explained sheepishly. "I was going to come back as soon as I was done checking on them. Honest."

Mr. Thomas put his hand on Max's shoulder. "Look, Son, I know you want to save that hive, and I see that you really care about this. Don't let it get you into trouble with us, okay?"

"Yes, Dad. I'm sorry I left the house without asking."

"We forgive you," said Mr. Thomas. "Now, go upstairs to

your room. You will be there for the rest of the day. We'll call you down when it's time to eat."

Max trudged upstairs to his room, cleaned up, and flopped onto his bed.

After a short while, Dex came in through the window. "Tank told me everything. It was Tank's idea to swarm the landscaper to distract him. The queen said that was a noble thing you did, approaching the hive. She said it took a lot of courage to risk getting stung just to save them."

"Really?" marveled Max.

"Yes, really. You made quite an impression on her."

"Wow, that's awesome!" said Max excitedly.

"How did it go with your parents?"

"Not too bad. I'm stuck in my room for the rest of the day."

"Did you tell them you got stuck and almost got ran over by a lawnmower?" Dex asked.

"I absolutely did not," Max said. "My parents would have completely lost it if I told them that."

"Max, I owe you an apology. I stood in the way of something you believed in, like approaching the hive. It was out of the ordinary, just like when I wanted to befriend you, and the hive was against it. I'm sorry, Max."

"Aw, that's okay, Dex," said Max. "Everything worked out for the better, right? Your hive has a few more days to prepare. That's all that matters. Now we just have to wait for the beekeeper to take the hive to the farm."

# CHAPTER FIFTEEN

## AFTERNOON PICKUP

Max and Dex sat quietly in the room, both deep in thought about the hive. Max wondered if the queen would let Dex back into the hive after they moved to the farm. Dex thought about the same thing, but he didn't want to be so far away from Max.

"Do you think the queen will let you back in the hive after the move?" Max finally asked.

"I don't know."

"What if she asked you to come back? Would you?"

"I honestly don't know," Dex shrugged. "I really do miss the hive, but I enjoy being around you. I would miss you so much if I moved to the farm with the hive."

"I would miss you too," Max said. "I could visit my grandparents just to see you, but it wouldn't be like how it is now. I would rather you stay with me."

"You would?"

"Yes. I don't want you to go. You are the greatest friend anyone could ask for. Sometimes I forget that you are a bee."

Dex smiled. "I don't even see you as a human anymore. I only see a friend."

Max laughed. "I would give you a hug, but you are too

small."

***

Later that afternoon, Max called the beekeeper to make sure he was still coming. Although Max had bought the hive a few extra days to get ready, he didn't want to wait until the last minute.

The beekeeper confirmed with Max that he would be there to pick up the hive the next afternoon. Max then told Dex, who then told Tank, who told the queen.

The queen told her hive to prepare for the move. Some of the bees were excited about the move; others were nervous. However, they all knew they had to move.

Tank had mixed feelings about moving to another hive. He had grown up here and loved everything about his home. He was going to miss the neighborhood, the foraging, and the field—but he was also curious about the farm. He wondered how it was going to be living there. He had only heard Dex explain it briefly, but Dex had sounded so excited about it. Tank was a little unsure about the humans taking care of them, but at this point, there were no other options to choose from.

***

Finally, the big day arrived. The beekeeper showed up around three in the afternoon. Max and Dex stood off in the distance and watched as the man put on his white suit, his netted mask, and his gloves. The landscapers showed up as well. They needed to cut the rest of the grass in the field.

"Okay, everyone needs to stay back," ordered the beekeeper. "These bees will be very angry."

"No they won't," said Max. "The bees will not attack. Just watch and see."

The beekeeper smiled. "Kid, I've been doing this for a long time. Trust me. I know the behavior of bees. They do not like to be disturbed."

Max smiled back at the beekeeper. "Trust me. I know those bees. They will not attack. This will be the easiest hive you have ever handled."

The beekeeper brought out his ladder, his bee smoker to calm the bees, and a box with breathing holes in it to put the hive in. As he drew close to the hive, he noticed there was not a single bee coming out to attack him. The beekeeper turned and gave Max a confused look. "You sure this hive has bees in it?" he asked.

"Positive," Max replied.

The beekeeper climbed up the ladder and placed both hands on the hive. He could feel the hive buzzing and humming in his hands, but still no bees came out to attack. The beekeeper looked at Max with bewilderment.

Max flashed the beekeeper with a wide, toothy grin. "See—I told you."

"Do I need the smoker?" the beekeeper asked sarcastically.

"Hmmm, I don't think so," Max replied.

The beekeeper shook his head and continued. He gently took the hive out of the tree and placed it in the box. He climbed down the ladder with the box and set it in the back seat of the truck. Then he told the landscapers it was safe to finish their job, and soon they were cutting the rest of the tall grass.

Max walked over to the beekeeper. "Thank you for coming out."

"Thank *you,* kid," said the beekeeper. "Our farm can always use extra bees to pollinate our crops and flowers. You can come and visit them anytime you want." He got into his truck, slowly drove off, and gradually picked up the speed so he wouldn't disturb the hive.

“Do you think you could get your dad to take you to the farm one more time?” Dex asked Max as they watched the beekeeper drive off with the hive.

“I don’t know. We just went to the farm a few days ago, but I'll ask him.”

“I hope they will like the farm like I did.”

“I’m sure they will love it there,” Max assured Dex. “That place is huge, and there are a lot of fruits and vegetables and different types of flowers to pollinate. Let’s go home.”

“I’ll race you!” shouted Dex, and he quickly flew away. “No fair! You got a head start!” yelled Max. He picked up his bike and pedaled quickly after Dex.

# CHAPTER SIXTEEN

## GOODBYE

The next morning, Max spoke to his dad before he went off to work. "Hey, Dad. Can we go to the farm again?"

"You have got to be kidding me," Mr. Thomas moaned. "You want to go the farm *again?*"

"Just to see the bees," said Max. "We don't have to take the tour again. The beekeeper said I can visit anytime I want."

Mr. Thomas rolled his eyes emphatically and sighed deeply. "Max, I am all farmed out."

"We're going to the farm again to see the bees, Daddy?" Joanna called from upstairs.

"Yes," Mr. Thomas sighed.

Mrs. Thomas, who was sitting in the living room, heard the conversation. "They are so ambitious," she said, laughing at her husband.

Mr. Thomas smiled back. "Too ambitious."

***

The queen and the bees were nervous as they huddled together on their way to the farm. They were in a box, in a truck, and they were trusting a human; all things they never could have imagined. The queen tried her best to keep her bees calm, but she was just as nervous as they were. The ride seemed to take forever.

Tank, however, was not nervous. He was going to be the first bee to come out to survey the area, then he was going to let the hive know when it was all clear to come out. He was going to attack the first human he saw. Tank had let his previous thoughts about humans consume him, and he was primed for attack.

The beekeeper finally arrived at the farm. He climbed out the truck, carefully picked up the box, and took the hive to the back. After donning his protective gear, he carefully opened the box.

Tank, who was ready to attack, flew out and landed on the beekeeper's netted mask. Tank stung repeatedly, but he couldn't get to the beekeeper's face.

"Calm down, little fella," the beekeeper soothed. "I'm not going to hurt you."

Tank kept jabbing his stinger into the netted mask but the beekeeper only smiled. He then took out a brand new, unused beehive. Tank finally realized his stinging was useless against his mask. He jumped off and landed on the new hive to inspect it. It was very spacious, neat, and clean. In fact, Tank thought this hive was better than their old hive.

Tank glanced around and saw other hives that looked like the one he was inspecting. He noticed the other bees leaving and entering their hives; they appeared to be happy living here. Tank lowered his guard and calmed down. He flew back to the old hive to let the queen know that the coast was clear.

All the bees in the hive surrounded the queen and carefully came out the box. After several minutes, all the bees were in their new hive.

The beekeeper watched from a distance. He wanted to make sure the bees were comfortable, and he didn't want to disturb them. After the bees had settled in, the beekeeper returned to them. “There, isn’t that better?” he asked. “You guys are going to love this place.”

“What do you think so far?” asked Tank after the beekeeper left the building.

The queen looked around and inspected the new hive. Then she went outside with an escort and searched the immediate area and returned a few minutes later, clearly impressed. "A queen can get used to this. I like it so far."

"The beekeeper appears to be genuinely nice like Max," Tank observed. "This might be a good place for us to live."

***

Trint saw the bees moving in and couldn't wait to meet them. When he saw that they had settled in, he flew over to greet them. "Hello, everyone," he greeted. "My name is Trint. I'm the lead forager for my hive, and I want to be the first to welcome you to the farm."

"Thank you," said the queen. "We look forward to working together with the other hives."

"Who is your lead forager?" asked Trint.

"We don't have a lead forager," replied the queen.

"You are going to need one. This place is huge. I can help train the one you appoint, Your Majesty."

The queen turned and looked directly at Tank. "I appoint you," she said.

Tank's expression turned to surprise. "What? You want *me* to be the lead forager?"

"Yes," the queen confirmed. "You have demonstrated yourself to be a true leader over the past few months. I especially saw your leadership skills when you took charge and saved Max back at the field. This position will be perfect for you to continue to improve."

"Thank you, Your Majesty," said Tank. "I will not let you down."

Trint approached Tank. "I will be here bright and early tomorrow to show you around and get you started. You are going to love it here!"

"I know," said Tank. "Everybody keeps saying that."

***

The next day, Mr. Thomas brought Max and Joanna to the farm. The kids jumped out of the car and raced toward the beekeeper's building.

Dex was in his usual place under Max's shirt collar. "I'll meet you at the lemon tree in about an hour," said Dex. When it was clear, Dex left Max's collar and headed to the hives. When he arrived, he ran into a minor problem: he didn't know which hive was his—they all looked the same. After a few minutes of looking, however, he spotted Brandon walking along the top of one of the hives.

"There they are," said Dex. He flew down toward Brandon. "Hey, how's it going, Brandon? How do you like it so far?"

"Meh, I'll get used to it," Brandon replied plainly.

"Where's Tank?"

"He's getting trained by some bee named Trint."

"I know Trint!" Dex exclaimed excitedly. "What is Tank getting trained for?"

"The queen appointed Tank as our first ever lead forager."

"Wow! That is awesome!" said Dex. "I'm meeting Max at the lemon tree in a bit. Wanna come?"

"Nope," said Brandon. "I'm staying put right here. I want to meet some of the other bees."

"Okay," said Dex. "I'll see you later."

The queen came out shortly after Dex flew away. "Was that Dex?" she asked.

"Yes," Brandon replied. "He went to the lemon tree to meet with the human."

"Drat! I wanted to talk to him," said the queen. "Oh well, that can wait for now. I need you to come inside quickly. I'm working on something special."

***

Dex met with Max at the lemon tree and quickly filled up on the lemon nectar. "Aaahhh, so refreshing and delicious," he said.

"How are the bees?" asked Max.

"Everyone seems to be settling in," Dex replied. "This place will be very good for them. Thank you, Max, for helping my hive get here."

"That's what friends are for." Max looked past Dex and saw a black cloud of insects heading directly toward them. "Dex, what is that?" he asked nervously.

Dex turned around and saw the cloud. "It looks like a

swarm of bees."

"Please tell me it's your hive, Dex."

"I can't tell from here. I'll go check."

"You do that, Dex. I'll hide behind this tree."

Dex quickly flew toward the swarm, and as he got closer, he realized it *was* his hive.

The queen spotted Dex flying toward them, and she commanded the swarm to halt. She came out the middle of the swarm to talk to Dex.

"What are you doing swarming out here, Your Majesty?" asked Dex.

"We have a little surprise for Max," the queen explained. "We have prepared something for him to show our gratitude for saving us and helping us find our new home."

Dex looked at the queen and the rest of the bees in amazement. "Are you going to talk to him?"

"Absolutely not!" laughed the queen. "We'll leave that for you to do."

Dex smiled. "Okay, let me go back to tell him it's alright. He thinks you are an angry swarm." Dex quickly flew back to Max, assuring him that it was ok, and that the bees wanted to show him something.

Max slowly crept out from behind the tree and stood up facing the swarm of bees. The bees drew closer to Max, then they formed into a tight bee ball, about the size of a basketball. Half of the bees then broke off from the bee ball and took the form of a human hand. The bees, shaped like a hand, slowly flew close to Max.

"I think the bees want a handshake," Dex said in awe.

Max slowly extended his hand to the "bee hand." The bee hand formed a grip with Max's hand, and they shook.

"This is unbelievable!" Max exclaimed.

After Max finished shaking hands with the bees, all of them flew back a few feet and formed the words: ***THANK YOU, MAX!***

"You're welcome," Max said. "You bees are awesome!"

The swarm then headed back to the hive, but the queen stayed behind with two escorts and approached Dex.

Max, sensing that she wanted to talk to Dex privately, walked a few feet away, sat on one of the benches, and watched.

"I want to thank you, Dex, for opening my blind eyes," said the queen. "I didn't trust humans because of what they did to our hive when I was a young bee. I let my disdain for humans spill over to this hive after I became queen."

Dex was shocked at what the queen was saying but kept quiet so she could continue.

"It took a courageous, ambitious, curious, and trustworthy bee to soften my heart toward humans. You have shown not only me, but also the entire hive, that not all humans are bad. You have proven me wrong, Dex. I banned you, and yet you still showed your loyalty to us by saving this hive. I am lifting your ban. You can come home."

Dex could not believe it. He could come back to the hive. He had dreamed of this moment. He then turned to Max and flew over to him. "The queen said my ban is lifted and I can come back home, but I still want to stay with you."

Max shook his head. "No, Dex. As much as I would love for you to come back home with me, you belong here with your family." Max had tears welling up in his eyes. "Your hive needs you, and I would be selfish to keep you to myself. Your place is here."

Dex was fighting back his own tears. He hated hearing what Max was saying to him, but he knew Max was right. Dex needed his hive, and his hive needed him. He flew in closer to Max and extended his front leg out to him. Max extended his index finger and they shook. "This is not goodbye, my bee friend," Max said.

"I learned so much from you," Dex said. "I have gained another best friend in you. I always knew something good would come out of this. I just didn't know that it would turn out to be this great."

Max, wiping away his tears, nodded in agreement. "I love you, Dex."

"I love you too, Max."

The queen and both escorts were now wiping away tears as they listened to Dex and Max.

Joanna ran up to Max. "Max, it's time to go home," she said, out of breath. "Hi, Dex, and bees I don't know."

Dex laughed. "Joanna, I want to thank you for helping us find a home and for not killing me."

"You're welcome, Dex," Joanna said proudly. Joanna looked at Max and saw that he was wiping away tears. "You are not coming back with us, huh?" she asked Dex.

"I'm afraid not," Dex replied. "I belong here with my hive."

Joanna lowered her head and began to cry. "But I just got to know you."

"I know. But you and Max can always visit. This is not goodbye forever."

"Yeah, but you are not living with us anymore," Joanna said. "I'm gonna miss you, Dex."

"I'm gonna miss you too, Joanna."

A car horn honked in the distance. It was Mr. Thomas. Dex landed on Max's shoulder and Max gently placed his hand over Dex. "Our first hug and I didn't get smooshed," Dex joked. Max laughed.

Dex quickly flew over to Joanna and landed on her shoulder. Joanna gently placed her hand on top of Dex just as she'd seen her big brother do.

"Take care of your brother, okay?" Dex said.

"Okay," Joanna sobbed.

Max and Joanna headed back to the car. Dex and the two escorts accompanied the queen back to the hive.

"Looks like you made quite the impression on them," the queen observed.

"They made an impression on me as well. I'm really going to miss them, especially Max."

"I know you will," said the queen. "Well, it looks like the Zoom and Boom Connection is going to be back in business!"

"Yes—I can't wait to tell Tank when he gets back."

# CHAPTER SEVENTEEN

## NEW ENCOUNTERS

A month went by. Dex and the hive blended in seamlessly with the other hives on the farm. Tank flourished as the lead forager; he appointed Dex as his lead assistant, and the quality of their honey improved significantly. With all the crops and flowers available, they came up with dozens of types of hints to their honey. Even the beekeeper noticed the different tastes.

The queen visited the other queens. She had a booming social life and didn't even have to go far to visit. Life was good once again for the hive . . . except for Dex.

Dex was now homesick in an unusual way. He missed Max's room. He missed the black suede ring box with the four cotton balls stuffed in it. He missed watching Max brush his teeth, even though he still thought it was gross. He missed hiding inside of Max's collar. He even missed Joanna.

Tank tried to cheer Dex up. He understood the bond between Dex and Max all too well. He and Dex shared the same bond as best friends.

Dex was sitting in his quarters when Tank came by for a

visit.

"Dex," Tank said. "I heard a new hive just arrived today. Want to come out and see them?"

"Not really."

"Come on, Dex. A new hive means new friends!"

"New hive, new friends," Dex repeated with a sigh.

"Okay, that's it! We are going outside right now!" Tank exclaimed. He grabbed Dex by the wings and pulled him outside. "It's time for you to cheer up."

While they were outside, Brandon flew over and joined them. "Hey, guys. The new hive is here. The beekeeper is bringing them over right now."

"Nice. We've got front row seats," said Tank.

The beekeeper brought the box over and set it on the table, then pulled out the new hive. He placed it right next to Dex and Tank's hive and stepped away. Within a few minutes, the new bees slowly crept out to look around.

Dex watched with boredom, until one bee caught his compound eyes. She was a forager just like him. She looked back, smiled at him, and flew into the new hive.

Dex perked up and fanned his wings in excitement. "Tank, did you see her?"

"See who?"

"The female bee! She was beautiful!"

"Dex, there are plenty of female bees. Which one are you

talking about?"

"Never mind." Dex flew back to the hive.

Later, just before sunset, Dex flew out of the hive to get some fresh air. He sat on top of his box hive and looked at the trees swaying in the summer wind.

"Hello," said an unfamiliar voice.

Dex looked behind him and spotted the female bee he saw earlier.

"Hi, my name is Z," she introduced.

"I'm Dex," he replied nervously. "What does Z stand for?" "Z is short for Zip, because I fly fast."

"Oh, really? I can fly fast too!"

"Is that so?" asked Z. "Wanna race?"

"I thought you'd never ask," Dex said with a smirk. "The apple tree—first one there wins."

"Sounds good," said Z. "Of course, I'll be at the apple tree way before you get there."

Both bees lined up to start the race and focused on the apple tree several yards away.

"On your mark . . . get set . . . go!"

Both bees took off! Dex held a slim lead over Z. Halfway through the race, Z took the lead. Dex caught up and both bees were even, heading into the final stretch of the race. Just before they reached the tree, Z pulled away and she won by a very slim margin.

"Wow, you are really fast!" Dex exclaimed.

Z caught her breath. "I told you I was. But you are the fastest bee I've ever raced."

Dex and Z stared at each other. They both knew that they liked each other, and they had something in common: they both loved to fly fast. Suddenly, Dex did not feel so homesick. Z made it all go away.

Soon enough, Dex and Z were foraging together, and Tank was back to foraging with Brandon. Tank didn't mind at all; he was just glad his best friend was happy again.

Dex and Z raced every day. Sometimes Z would win; sometimes Dex would win. Soon, other bees from other hives would join the race. Dex or Z would finish first or second, and it wasn't even close for the other bees. Dex and Z were the fastest bees on the farm.

Early one morning, Dex and Z were on their break from foraging. "So what's your story?" Dex asked. "How did your hive end up here?"

"We outgrew our hive, so half of us had to leave," said Z. "We ended up swarming in a back yard. The humans that lived there called a beekeeper to get us. It turned out good because he brought us here."

"Nice," said Dex.

"So, what's your story?" Z asked.

"My story is longer than yours," Dex warned.

"I've got time to listen," Z said.

"Okay, here goes. It started with me being stuck in a spider's web, and then a human boy saved me from the spider that was about to "drink" me. I was so grateful, I decided to follow him home and actually speak to him and say thank you. We became friends, and then I was kicked out the hive because I showed him the hive, so I ended up moving in with him. Later, I found out my hive was in danger due to construction. The human that saved me helped to get us here. My queen then lifted my ban because I helped to get them here . . . Whew, that was a lot, huh?"

"Wow, you actually spoke to a human?" asked Z in amazement.

"Yes, I did. If I hadn't followed him home to talk to him, we wouldn't be here today."

"And I would have never met you," Z added. Dex blushed. "Okay, time to get back to work." Z laughed. "Okay, okay . . . I'll stop being mushy."

***

Max tried his best to take his mind off Dex. He missed him so much. He no longer wore his collar shirts anymore; there was no need to since Dex wasn't around to hide in them. Max was back to wearing T- shirts.

He constantly looked at Dex's ring box bed he'd made for him. He missed talking to Dex at night after bedtime. He missed taking him on trips with his family. He missed teaching him what humans did. *Who is going to replace Dex's friendship?* he wondered.

Sometimes Max would take his bike and ride to the field where Dex used to live and watch the construction workers. The field was unrecognizable now. The tall grass and the trees were no longer there; metal beams and concrete had taken their place. Huge cranes and bulldozers slowly moved back and forth, hard at work.

After a while, Max became bored watching the construction workers and began to head home. He passed a softball field on his way and saw some kids playing a pick-up game of softball. As he passed them, two of the kids flagged Max down.

"Hey! We're a player short. Do you want to play with us?"

"Sure," Max said.

"My name is Kevin, and this is my brother, Nathan."

"I'm Max." Max shook hands with Kevin and Nathan, and then they introduced Max to the rest of the players.

"I don't have a glove," said Max.

"I have a bag full of gloves," said Nathan. "I got righties and lefties. Take your pick."

Max picked out his glove and they began to play. He played several games and played very well. Before he knew it, several hours had passed, and his curfew was fast arriving.

"I gotta go, guys," said Max. "Are you playing tomorrow?"

"Yup," Kevin replied. "Good game today. Come back tomorrow."

Max hopped onto his bike and rode home. For a few hours, he forgot about how much he missed Dex. He also found some potential friends to hang out with. *Maybe Kevin and Nathan are just the guys to help me ease the sting of not having my best friend around,* Max thought. He would have to figure all of that out gradually.

# CHAPTER EIGHTEEN

## UNTIL NEXT SPRING

NATURE'S AUTUMN SONG: The summer gave the autumn permission to take over. Autumn immediately made its presence felt. The days were now getting shorter, and the September breeze was chillier; autumn had arrived. The birds were starting their annual journey south in pursuit of warmer weather. V-shaped flocks began to fill the skies; autumn had arrived. The green leaves in the trees gradually were replaced with colors of orange, gold, and crimson. Their grand finale had begun. Soon the ground would be littered with colorful fallen leaves; autumn had arrived. Chipmunks and squirrels were no longer darting up and down trees harvesting food. The hibernating season was upon them, for autumn had arrived.

Max and Dex had adjusted quite well since the last time they'd seen each other. Max had made new friends in Kevin and Nathan. They now played flag football on Saturday mornings at the park. Max even had them over his house sometimes to play video games. *Dex would be so proud of me,* Max thought.

Sometimes, Max would wonder if he would be friends with Kevin and Nathan if Dex was still living with him.

*Probably not,* he thought to himself. Although Max missed Dex terribly, he knew at some point that he was going to have to have friends other than a bee.

Dex loved life at the farm. He was happy that the hive enjoyed living here as well. Everything had turned out the way he'd envisioned it when he'd first come to the farm.

Dex and Z had grown close in their relationship; they were nearly inseparable, spending as much time together as they could.

In a few days, all the bees would be living exclusively in their respective hives for the entire fall and the winter months to avoid the cold. Some of the hives at the farm had already begun their "turn in" for the fall.

Dex still missed Max, and he wished he could see him one more time before the turn in, but he thought that was very unlikely. Max was already back in school, and the bees only had a few days before they would begin their turn in for the cold months.

The entire farm was prepared for autumn: All the crops were harvested, the animals were moved into the big barn to avoid the cold ahead, and most of the festivity attractions and supplies were put away for the summer. At that time of the year, very few people visited the farm. This was the last week before the farm was closed to the public.

"What are the odds that Max comes to visit before we turn in?" asked Tank.

"I don't know," replied Dex. "I'm not expecting him to come until the spring."

"I know for a fact Max will be the first one here come spring," said Tank. "It would be nice to see him again before the turn in."

***

The next day, Tank was out flying around the apple orchard by himself. He was going to be inside the boxed hive for several months, so he wanted to enjoy the last few days of being outside in the beautiful, cool weather before the turn in. He rested on one of the branches in the apple tree and took several deep breaths. "Aaaaaaahhhhh—the air here is so much cleaner and fresher than at the neighborhood," he said to himself. "This is so-o-o relaxing."

As Tank was relaxing, he saw a car pull up at the entrance to the farm. An older man got out of the car, the farmer came out, and they shook hands. A boy was with the older man, but Tank couldn't see who it was because the people were too far away.

"That's not Max," said Tank. He then closed his eyes and began to relax again.

"Dex, where are you?" shouted a voice in the distance. Tank looked around to see who was calling Dex. The voice was faint, so Tank couldn't recognize it. He thought it was Z at first, but then he remembered that her hive had already turned in for the fall and winter.

"Dex, are you still here?" asked the voice.

Tank looked and saw Max running toward the lemon trees. Tank quickly flew back to the hive to tell Dex.

"Dex!" Tank cried as he flew. "Max is here! Max is here!" Tank arrived at the hive. "Where is Dex?"

"He's in his quarters," snapped Brandon. "Stop all that hollering!"

Tank quickly flew to Dex's quarters and barged in. "Dex," Tank said out of breath. "Didn't you hear me?"

"No," Dex replied.

"Max is here!" shouted Tank. "He's really here!"

A surprised look came over Dex's face. "Where is he?" "By the lemon trees!" Tank cried excitedly.

Dex was out of his quarters before Tank finished saying "lemon trees." When Dex made it outside, he could hear Max calling him. He flew faster than he ever had in his entire life. He finally made it to the lemon tree and saw Max. "Max, you're back!"

"Did you really think I was going to let you turn in and not let me see you before the spring?" Max laughed. "I know how much you raved about the lemon nectar, so I figured I would find you here."

"I am so glad to see you."

"I had to see you one more time before the turn in," said Max. "Spring is a long time from now."

"I didn't think your dad was going to bring you out here

again."

"He wasn't," said Max, laughing. "My grandfather bought Joanna and I some back-to-school supplies, and my dad had to come and get them. Luckily, I didn't have school today, so I came along. My grandfather is very good friends with the farmer, so I convinced him to bring me here so he can catch up with his old friend. Dad wanted to stay behind, so he's waiting on us to get back."

Tank arrived a short time later. "Is that Tank?" asked Max.

"Yup, that is him," said Dex proudly. "He's the Boom in the Zoom and Boom Connection."

"Wow, he's big!" Max observed.

"Hence, the Boom," joked Dex.

"I'm assuming he's here for you," said Max.

Tank looked to his left, and then he quickly looked to his right, and he took a deep breath and spoke fast, in one breath. "Hi, Max. Thank you for saving us. We love it here. Dex, don't tell anyone I spoke to him. Gotta go. Bye, Max. See you next spring!" Tank smiled and quickly flew back to the hive.

Max and Dex were left speechless, but then shared a laugh.

"Tank was really bummed out because he wasn't there to participate in the epic 'bee-hand' handshake," Dex explained. "I guess he wanted to do something 'epic.'"

“Wow, he actually spoke to me.” Max shook his head in disbelief. “I don’t know which of you talking to me was more surprising: you or Tank.”

“Me,” said Dex, with a smile. “I spoke to you first. You will never forget that.”

Max and Dex spent the last hour or so reminiscing about the first day they’d met, how they’d become good friends, and the adventures they’d both had together and individually. They never would have gotten to this point if Max had ignored a muffled buzz in a spider’s web.

Max and Dex could see positive changes in one another. There would be no need to ask each other about the new friends they made. This moment belonged to Dex and Max. Besides, they had the spring to talk about their new friends.

Max’s grandfather called for him to get ready to go. “I guess this is it,” said Max.

Dex and Max shared a brief embrace. “See you next spring, my friend,” said Dex.

“I’ll meet you at the lemon tree.” Max waved and ran back to his grandfather, and Dex flew back to the hive.

This was not the sad goodbye of a few weeks earlier. This was more of a “see you later” kind of goodbye.

Max and Dex, a human boy and a honeybee, had formed an unlikely bond over the summer that would never be broken. Theirs was an unusual friendship, built on one’s open-mindedness and one’s willingness to step outside the boundaries because of something he believed in. Together, they not only saved the hive, but they gained the respect of those affected by their friendship.

Joanna no longer killed insects that were inside the house. Instead, she captured them and released them outside—far from the house, of course.

The queen, inspired by the friendship between Dex and Max, put Dex in charge of teaching the hive how to interact with humans—mainly the beekeepers on the farm.

Dex's hive finally turned in for the fall and winter months. Later that night, Dex lay in his quarters, taking in all of what the summer offered him. Thanks to Max, he had access to the best tasting honey ever made by his hive. His hive also had a better appreciation for humans, thanks to Max's selfless act to rescue them.

Max lay in his bed looking at Dex's ring box bed. He smiled, thinking about how disgusted Dex had been when he'd seen Max brushing his teeth for the first time. Max had a new respect and appreciation for insects.

Neither of them had ever thought in a million years that they would have a friendship like the one they shared together. They both thought about the future adventures that they would have together, the new places yet to be seen and the people and the insects they would encounter together. Thinking about this made them both excited and eager. They would have to be patient, because this would have to wait—until next spring.

# ABOUT THE AUTHOR

A.R. Johnson, author of Victor Storey and future author of BeeFriend Two, is a U.S. Air Force veteran, who wrote his first story while in elementary school. He, in time, would have a dream that would later become the book you are currently reading. He also was inspired by a classic childhood book that involved a pig and a spider. Now a full-time writer, A.R. Johnson currently resides in Illinois with his beautiful wife and daughter.